THE INVISIBLE

STEVE STRED

BLACK VOID PUBLISHING

Edited by David Sodergren

Cover by A.A. Medina, Fabled Beast Design

Foreword by Jeremy Hepler

Ebook ISBN: 9781990260438

Paperback ISBN: 9781990260445

Ingram Paperback ISBN: 9781990260452

Foreword by Jeremy Hepler

When I read 'The Invisible' five years ago (titled 'Invisible' back then) and was introduced to Steve Stred's writing for the first time, I knew within in the first few pages I'd discovered an author who was a natural at connecting with readers. An author who had the proverbial ability to bleed onto the page, pour their heart and soul and experience into their words. To say I was a fan of his storytelling from the get-go would be an understatement.

Not only were Steve's various settings in Invisible magnetic, pulling me in so close and tight that each time I stopped reading it took a second for me to remember where I really was, his characters also possessed a sense of comfort and familiarity that made me feel as though I'd known them my entire life. The first-person narrator felt like an old friend, a neighbor, a family member, someone I cared about and understood. I shared in their dread, confusion, desperation, relief, all of it, as the story unfolded, and the heart-wrenching truth was revealed in a series of linked memories and dreams. I finished the story in two days, thought about it daily for a week or more afterward, and later, after I learned huge chunks of it were autobiographical, revisited certain scenes with a different understanding.

So, when Steve told me he was going to fine-tune 'The Invisible' for a rerelease and asked if I would be willing to write a foreword, I jumped at the opportunity. I'll admit, with so little time and so many new novels and authors out there to explore nowadays, and with my natural preference to go into stories totally blind, I'm usually reluctant to reread any longer works, but I knew this story would be an exception. I couldn't wait to see how he'd enhanced it. I sped through it in one sitting the second time around and was just as enthralled with the narrator's physical, mental, and emotional journey as I was the first time. (Sorry to be so vague, but I don't want to give away any details that could ruin the experience of peeling back the layers of this one on your own.). The subtle improvements Steve has made, and the fact that his writing skills have been honed to a fine edge over the last half decade, have helped tighten up the story without removing any of the substance. I could still easily smell his blood on each page.

Revisiting 'The Invisible' was a pleasant reminder that every time I dive into one of Steve's longer works (I've read most if not all of them at this point.), I know the adventure I'm about to embark on will make me smile and laugh, gasp and shudder, and often, like the last few pages of this one, bring me to tears.

If this is a reread for you, too, I hope you enjoy the second time around as much as I did.

And if you've never read The Invisible before, buckle up. You're in for a fantastic ride.

Jeremy Hepler
July 19, 2024

For Nanny, Auntie Cheryl,
And those who've left this world far too soon.

X.

The rolling hills tumbled down to mossy rocks that eventually flattened and faded, lining the edge of a winding road made of old cobblestone. To the left, a valley narrowed, a river cascading down until it caressed the waters it fed. The expanse was a few hundred meters wide, the opposite side jutting straight up, an unclimbable wall of a thousand feet, before growing jagged and forming one side of the mountain range. Back on the mainland, the road continued to undulate, stopping at the base of the Lighthouse. Standing one hundred feet tall, with a glass dome on top, the Lighthouse had stood in this spot for 150 years. Off to the right, the water stretched out farther than the eye could see. Directly in front of the structure, blue waves smashed onto a rocky shoreline, which over the years had seen its fair share of close calls. But every close call had only been a close call because of the Lighthouse. From further back, the Lighthouse resembled an old barber shop wheel. But as travelers approached, its features became distinct, eliciting gasps as its grandeur appeared. Over the years, many people had the privilege of manning the Lighthouse, but the last few years had seen that figure diminish. Where once twenty-twenty five boats of all sizes would pass daily, now five sailed by in a week. But saving five boats from a watery grave amongst the rocks was worth having it run all day, every day. The town had maintained its grounds, though there was very little to do, and had ensured that the paint remained fresh and that the light never wavered.

It beat the alternative of appearing abandoned, and having local youth cover it with graffiti, breaking the windows and using the dome to get high. Soon, though, the town was abandoned, and the Lighthouse empty, the last sentry guarding the gates to the Promised Land having departed. Weeks seemed to merge into months, years into decades. While nobody occupied the building, the calendar inside continued to track the days, pages flipping in a soft breeze, waiting for something ancient to appear once more.

XX.

It lay dormant for years.

The Beast.

Waiting to be unleashed and devour its way through the world.

Laying waste to everything in its path.

The trees rustled, as a slow, lazy breeze blew through the woods, building in intensity until it howled in the distance.

Unperturbed, the Beast remained in a tight ball of fur and fury.

In the distance, a hum found the Beast's ears.

Its breathing increased.

Its nose twitched, its muscles tensed, and its hatred unfurled.

1.

The realization that I was lost and about to run out of gas made me slam my hands on the steering wheel. I started to curse, but instead choked on an inadvertent hunk of spit I'd inhaled, the act causing me to break into laughter.

Choke to death on my own spit, I thought. How ironic would that be?

Pulling to the side of the winding road, I took in the stunning view that surrounded me. From where I was parked, the water sparkled, and the hills danced in every direction.

A postcard picture view, I thought.

That is, until the town lost its main source of employment, and everyone moved away. In its place was a shuttered, dirt-strewn reminder of what used to be.

I was on my own out here, which was fine by me. It was what was necessary, all things considered. While for most, the decision would've been difficult, I knew it was the correct one, and I made it after careful consideration. Easing back onto the stone-covered road, I drove on. The condition of the road worsened the closer I got to the Lighthouse. The car jostled and bounced, which forced me to drive just off the edge where it was smoother, but also suggested the hazard of getting stuck in the soft ground. And if that happened, there'd be no way I could get the car free on my own.

I couldn't imagine taking a horse and wagon over this but judging from the depths of the ruts running in front of me, people did so for many years. Though, back then I'd assume the road was in better condition.

As the Lighthouse neared, it was hard to fathom the magnitude of what its purpose really was. *Saving lives.* Preventing boats from being crushed on the rocky shores. I'm not sure why I was drawn to this place. I only hoped it would reveal its secrets to me and tell me why.

But only when it was ready.

I pulled the car alongside the Lighthouse and put the car in park, the height of the building looming over me like the shadow of a god. Tilting my neck to see the top, I had a flashback to a summer in college when I worked as a window installer for a construction company. A new high rise was being built, and to place the big panes of glass correctly, you had to get into a bulky harness, lean way out over the edge of the building, and direct the glass panel into the appropriate slot while a crane operator delicately moved it into place.

I quit by lunch on day one.

Getting out of the car, I ignored how much dirt was caked on the sides – I'd wash it later – and retrieved my backpack from the rear seat. A decades-old path ran around the side, which I followed. I found an old wooden door. If I had to guess, I'd say it was original wood, but with updated hardware, judging by the shine of the door handle. Though it appeared new, it took a monstrous effort on my part to turn it. The door was far heavier than expected, though I should've expected that considering the age, and after only pushing it two inches, it ground to a halt, stuck in the frame. Bracing my feet on the ground, I pushed with all my strength, the door finally dislodging from its hold and opening with a bone-rattling shriek.

Stepping inside, I marveled at the old-world craftsmanship that greeted me in the small space. I could almost see the ghosts of Lighthouse Keepers past kicking off their wet boots as they hung up their rain-soaked coats. The place was surprisingly clean. At least, the entrance was. As my eyes adjusted to the dimness, I saw the room was about twenty feet across, and on the other side there was the beginning of a circular staircase that looped up to the higher floors.

"Hello?"

I was unsure why I hollered, but it felt like the right thing to do. As though I've stopped at a neighbor's home and found the front door open.

"Is there anybody here?"

Silence greeted my question, so I set my bag down on a bench beside me, confident I wouldn't startle some vagrant who'd decided this might be the perfect place to squat.

Wondering what surprises might await me higher up, I crossed the room and started up the stairs, wondering if it might give way and come tumbling down.

As my foot hit the metal step, a noise came from far above, echoing down.

For a second I swore that someone had called my name.

2.

"Hello?"

I called again as I arrived at the second floor.

When nothing called back, I looked around. The kitchen. It's as though time had stopped, and I'd stepped into the pages of a catalog from my youth. An ancient stove stared back at me; its dreary mustard color faded. 'It's been so long' it seemingly whispered.

Just a little longer, I wanted to whisper back. I'll use you soon.

I went over to the counter and cabinets, admiring the craftsmanship in their construction. They may be old, but they're ornate and still in pristine condition, a testament to how things were made before quantity over quality became the driving aspect of the business model. The fridge was medium sized, and peering in, the light popped on when I opened the door and a cool breeze of air hit me, which alleviated a stress I didn't fully know I had until that moment. If the fridge wasn't working, I'd be screwed, I realized. Knowing it'd be for the best if I went and retrieved my supplies from the car before heading higher, I still decided to postpone that act, curiosity over what awaited me further above outweighing going back outside so soon.

THUMP.

I jumped when the unexpected sound came from above.

THUMP.

It came again, almost instantly after the first impact, and louder this time, fuller.

A dread took hold, one that suggested I keep my mouth shut and turn tail and flee, but instead, my legs refused to move, and, like a dumbass, my mouth opened.

"Hello?"

My voice cracked as I spoke.

Silence.

Run, my brain screamed again. Run, run, run, run.

But even as I had that impulse, another thought rattled around inside my head.

Go. See. Investigate.

It's those thoughts that propelled me up the stairs, heading towards the third floor, not down to the main floor, where the door to my escape sat shut.

I was far calmer than I should be, a revelation that arrived once I reached the opening in the stairs that allowed me to exit to the third floor. It appeared, upon initial impressions, to be both the dining area and an entertainment space. Along the far wall a table sat, two empty plates and associated cutlery placed on the tabletop around them. On one corner of the table sat an empty fishbowl. No longer filled with water or home to any fish, it instead was decorated by a green growth that wrapped completely around the interior. Above it on the wall hangs a clock in the shape of a cat; black and white with big circular eyes and a tail hanging below. As the clock ticked, the tail swung back and forth. It's only after watching it for several seconds that I noticed the eyes moved in sync with the tail. The longer I stared at the eyes, the more it suggested the cat clock is annoyed with my presence. A calendar hung from the wall just below the clock and above the fishbowl. So perfectly placed to not touch either object, that even the thought of flipping it to the next month would cause an individual with OCD to spiral out of control. It was a two-piece calendar. The current photo was of three men, all shirtless, standing in front of a hut, that, based on the palm trees surrounding it, suggested it was taken in Hawaii. At their feet, on the sand, was some sort of fish. It looked to be about thirty feet long and four feet wide, and possessed a giant mouth. The caption below said, 'Caught off the coast, the creature weighed 800 lbs.' The calendar was dated April 1932. I examined the calendar closer and found some writing within the squares. Friday, April 21, had 'REVIEW' scrawled in blocky pen letters. Saturday, April 22 said, 'SS Night Child' and beside that in pen, '0-200,' which I guessed must refer to an early morning passing time of the previously mentioned boat.

On the opposite side of the room was an old green couch facing an empty shelving unit, which would seem like a place a small television might've sat. Overall, the room was sparse but usable and would work just fine for my needs.

THUMP.

The noise seemed to come from directly above me, so much so, that I instinctively ducked and covered my head. My knees and back reminded me that I'd been sitting for some time in the car earlier, and that their stiffness hadn't loosened up. I grimaced, rubbing my knees, and leaned back to stretch my hips as I stood. What the fuck was making that noise?

"Hello?"

Louder this time, an annoyance flavored my tone. If I ended up getting all the way to the top of the Lighthouse, only to find a flag flapping in the breeze, I'd have to seriously reconsider if this job was for me. If I got this scared from a random noise, how would I possibly stay here for any length of time?

Another THUMP sounded, and oddly, to my ears, it made me think it was an invitation, to continue seeking what was behind the noise.

3.

Disgusted by the decision I'd made, I'd thrown what fit into my backpack and left our apartment, not caring if I turned the lights off or locked the door behind me. Climbing into my black Volkswagen Golf, I shoved the key into the ignition, turned the car on, and backed out of my parking stall. The garage door took forever to open, but when it finally did, the rain outside was falling with a steady pattering as I pulled out of the underground garage and drove away. The rain had begun a few days earlier and had continued to grow in ferocity ever since. The car had recently been outfitted with new wipers, which according to the salesman, were designed to make my vision less obstructed no matter the volume of water against the window. I should've returned them and got my money back. No use now, as I doubted I'd ever be back. I weaved through the light traffic, exited onto the freeway, and as the lights of the city dimmed and disappeared in the mirror, the road darkened, and the rain increased its fierce assault on my eyes and ears.

The gas tank was full, and I had a simple desire to put everything as far behind me as possible and just drive. Where? I wasn't sure, but wherever I ended up was fine by me. Once that was decided, I felt a buoyancy I'd not felt in years. I flipped through the music on my phone until arriving at one of my favorite driving tunes. I cranked the volume, punched the gas, and felt the rear-end slide on the wet surface until the wheels finally caught, and the car lurched forward, a sly smile on my face.

Three hours later, I came to the proverbial fork in the road.

The rain had decreased, turning into a fine mist, a greyness taking hold of the surroundings. Zipping over a slight hill, I steered around a curve and had to slam on the brakes. I'd travelled this road dozens of times, and never once had this intersection been there.

This shouldn't exist.

Had I been so deep in thought that I'd made a wrong turn somewhere? I was confused.

Either way, here I was. Stopped at an intersection that only offered two options – left or right.

This unexpected intersection caused new anxiety. Why had I never seen this before?

My mind raced, and my breathing became heavy, as though I was about to hyperventilate, which wouldn't do me any good.

Big breath in, big breath out.

I forced myself to inhale, letting the exhale linger as it left my lungs. This technique had helped me a dozen times over the last number of months, and it certainly helped me in this instance.

Wump, Wump.

I'd forgotten about the wipers, still set on high even though the rain had almost completely dissipated, and when they whipped across the windshield, I jumped in my seat. "Jesus Christ," I said with a chuckle, feeling embarrassed, but glad there were no witnesses. The wipers crossed again, and I turned them off.

To my left, the road travelled between two open fields before disappearing into a valley. With the onset of dusk, the sun had dropped behind the mountains around me about an hour ago, and my initial anxiety had begun to subtly increase. With each moment sat at that intersection, it grew even more. I needed to decide which way to go, and I needed to decide ASAP. Looking to the left, the road was unpaved and marked with deep grooves and potholes. It was a stretch of road rarely traveled or maintained. Not far off, the road seemed to transform into a mixture of crumbled pavement and dirt patching, with a steep incline carrying it into a mountainous terrain that didn't scream 'scenic drive.' Where it disappeared into the trees, the white of snow could be seen dusting the tops of the trees, which only meant further up would be worse. Thinking back, I didn't remember seeing a road sign or marker that indicated the distance until the next town, nor were there any markers on how far until the next gas station. Usually, especially throughout these mountain passes, every few kilometers a sign would tell you how far away you were, or at the very least, you'd be reminded to get gas because the next fuel stop wasn't for hours. The heaviness in my chest ratcheted up further as I realized I had no idea how far away either of those things were.

Looking at the gas gauge, I could've sworn I'd had more than a quarter tank left when I'd pulled up to the intersection. This inched its way into my brain, putting more weight on which way I'd go. The left suggested it was the safer of the two. When I looked right, a memory flooded back that I hadn't thought of in years.

It was from when I was six, and I'd gone fishing with my dad.

I'd never been fishing before, so this excited me, but I was even more amped because it was with my dad. He was often busy working or doing whatever it was that adults did, which made me pine for his attention. When he got all his fishing gear together and tossed it in the truck, I thought for sure he'd give me a wave and off he'd go. Instead, he hollered at me and produced my very own fishing rod. I smiled so hard when he hoisted me into the truck, and then we left, my dad and me. We drove for an hour or so, which felt like forever when you could barely see over the dash. "We're getting close," he said, after I let out a big yawn. We dipped down a small hill, when a creek ahead came into view. It had the blackest water I'd ever seen. My dad huffed, as we slowed to a crawl, passing by a few other anglers who'd already set up shop before we arrived. "We'll need to move further up the creek," he said. We parked the old green truck with the slightly rusted tailgate, grabbed our rods and tackle box from the back, and made our way further from the others. I had no idea if my dad knew where we were going, or if he was purely looking for a spot that suited his fancy – though I was young, I knew fishermen were superstitious folk – so I just followed along, singing a song to myself and enjoying my time in his presence.

"There," my dad said after some time, pointing ahead. Even at that age, I realized the act of pointing was anticlimactic. *Of course*, I thought, *the bright spot by the water.*

That bright spot paid off.

We remained at that spot for hours. We fished, laughed, and carried on like this was what we always did. He showed me how to set my rod, get the hook knotted tight and how to cast. We caught some fish, and threw some back, '*for the rest downstream to catch*,' my dad informed me.

Soon enough, it was time to head home, and we packed up. As we walked back to the truck, me with my little fishing pole in hand, and my dad carrying his as well as the tackle box and fish we'd caught, he stopped and said, "You know, sometimes at work the only way you get through the boredom is thinking about days like today." I simply looked at my dad, this burly lumberjack of a man, and tried to process his sudden philosophical turn. When he said nothing else for a time, we continued, and I thought he'd finished sharing. But then he stopped again two dozen paces later and said, "Turned out it was good timing that those other folk were here before us. Who knows how our day would've gone if we'd not been forced to find a new place."

As I sat there trying to decide if I should go left or right, I knew, much like my dad back then, that I needed a sign to direct me towards where I should go. I didn't have a preference either way. The road to the left was paved, flat, and had no snow. Going over my mental checklist, I understood why I preferred that choice. *Boring, predictable, and safe.* Going to the right would give me difficulty, variation, and danger. I glanced at the only photo of *us* that I'd grabbed as I left, and I knew I needed to confront danger head on.

It was decided.

Right.

I turned in that direction, and for the next hour, I never looked back.

4.

Thump.

Nothing about that sound made any sense.

At least not in that moment.

And with each successive impact, I tried to tell myself it was an animal that somehow found its way in and was searching for a way out. Judging from the hardness of each impact, my brain also told me that it would need to be a bear to make a noise that loud. There remained a draw to go up, to seek and find what was making the noise. The staircase carried on above, like a winding roadway to a secret world. I put my foot on the first step to continue and fell with such force that I pitched forward and *WHAM!* My shin drove against the edge of the stairs. Excruciating pain shot up my leg, all the way to the base of my skull. I toppled backward, staggered to regain my balance, the horrific thought of tumbling down to the main floor head over heel on the hard steps enough to motivate me to windmill my hands and grab the railing. Using the rail to pull myself back to my feet, I rubbed my shin where it had hit the stairs but couldn't feel my leg. Instead, it was numb, and pain coursed up and down the limb. I shook the leg in a fruitless attempt to get it to 'wake up,' but this was far more than a case of sitting in a strange position for too long. For some odd reason, my whole leg was completely numb, and I was unable to put any weight on it.

At the same time, my left arm began to feel the same, my fingers going numb, and a pain shot through my elbow. I tried to lift my arm, to make a fist, but the appendage dangled, lifeless and unresponsive.

This isn't good.

I bored a hole in my arm with my eyes, as I glared at it and willed it to do something, anything.

But nothing happened.

Suddenly, my body fell forward as both legs gave out. Unable to stop it or even raise my arm in protection, my head cracked off the steps much like my shin had only moments ago.

WHAM!

Everything went foggy as blood poured down my forehead, over my eyes and nose. A blackness arrived as I slumped unconscious, sprawled on the stairs.

Sometime later, my arm throbbed, the pain strong enough to wake me.

Disoriented, a dried puddle of blood on the stairs was the first thing my eyes found. Unable to shift to my right, something hard pressed against me, preventing movement. I used my right arm to push away from the hard thing just enough for me to see it was a wall I was against. *Weird*, I thought, *my bed's not against a wall.*

'You're not at home.'

A strange, new voice filled my head, gruff and aged. It forcefully stated the obvious, but it did so with a hint of dread, and while the voice was unknown, I knew it was someone I'd never want to meet. I used my good arm to push myself, but this was met with excruciating pain down the left side of my body, which mercifully stopped halfway down my leg. I waited for it to come again, but when it didn't, I scooted away from the wall until I felt the edge of the stairs. I still didn't remember where I was. My head throbbed, most of my body numb, and I didn't know what these strange stairs were.

Come on, I begged myself. *Figure it out.*

Why only one side? Why did I have a throbbing headache, and why was there dried blood on the step? I shifted on the edge of the stair, which caused a burning sensation up and down my left leg. I wiggled my toes, rolled my ankle around, but still couldn't feel anything. *Did I fall down the stairs?*

'Get up, fool.'

That other voice. It was like a swarm of bees in my head, and hearing it forced me to my feet, numb leg be damned.

Relying on my right side, I grabbed the railing and pulled, as though doing a one-arm pull up. I managed to hoist myself enough to get my right leg under me and, by doing a single-leg squat, got up. My weight remained on my right leg; my body propped against the wall.

THUMP!

"What the fuck?" I said when the noise from above came. The feeling that I'd been in this predicament before took over. But when? The ever-growing lump on my forehead throbbed worse than my leg, but the wall gave me some security, something dependable to lean against.

The noise came again – *THUMP!* – which startled me so badly, I almost lost my balance. The noise seemingly came from above and below, the circular stairs amplifying the sound and creating confusion. *THUMP!* A round window a few feet away offered a vantage point I'd not noticed before, so I slid over, wincing as new pain flared down my body. The window was coated in a thick layer of scum, as though it had not been cleaned in years, if not decades. I managed to clear some of the grime away with my hand, exposing a large section of glass through which I looked out. There, my eyes found water. Lots of water. I could see a coastline ahead and, to the left, mountains. *A Lighthouse.* It was the only thing I could think of that would explain the clues that surrounded me. And as though somebody had flipped a switch in my brain, with the understanding of where I was, everything came back. I'd been exploring the floors, trying to find the source of that noise when I fell. But the one thing that I couldn't pinpoint was why a Lighthouse? My head hurt, and I was exhausted. I needed to sit and figure out what was wrong with me, and what I could even do, given my circumstances. Finding somewhere to sit would be the easy part. The floor that housed the living area would be ideal. There'd be a couch which sounded heavenly at that moment. Or, I could chance it and go higher, see if another level offered something more suitable. The thought of exploring further options didn't appeal to me, based on how tired I was. A couch would be perfect.

Unable to trust that my legs would carry my weight, I gingerly sat, and pulled myself across each step until I'd made it to the living room. It took far longer than it should've, and by the time I got there I was even more exhausted, but it was necessary to take my time and not fall again. Immediately, I noticed things had changed. The fishbowl was where it had been, but now it had water and within, two fish swam around. A TV was on a shelf where I knew one hadn't been before. *Maybe it had been, and I'd just not seen it?* No, that wasn't right, I remembered thinking that'd be a perfect place to put one.

From where I stood, the couch was five thousand miles away. At least with how my body felt, and the way the room was spinning. Thankfully the tightness in my neck had subsided. My left foot wasn't doing any better, which frustrated me, but not as much as how weak my arm was. It still hung limp from my shoulder, as though it'd become detached from my central nervous system. No matter, I told myself, we need to get to that couch. I shuffled slowly, right foot first, left foot after. Once they were together and I was balanced, I repeated. Right, pause. Left, pause. What would normally take seconds, took about ten minutes. Once I was a foot from the couch, a sudden, sharp pain blasted through my head, and a feeling like vertigo took over. Knowing I was fighting remaining conscious again, I got my shins against the edge of the couch and then let my body fall forward. Landing hurt, but I'd made it and that at least diminished some of the pain.

My eyes grew heavy as I fought against exhaustion, but before I drifted to sleep, I heard that harsh voice again. *'Maybe you should stay awake. Could be a concussion.'* I didn't know if there was any validity to the 'don't fall asleep after having a concussion' theory, but it didn't matter. I was far too tired to keep my eyes open, and nobody else was here to keep me awake. As my eyes closed, a thought poked through. *Had there been a red coffee cup on the table?*

Without knowing the answer to that, I drifted off, sleep welcoming me in no time.

5.

As the summit approached, I began to think maybe I'd made the wrong decision.

Maybe I should've gone in the other direction and taken my chances?

Surprisingly, for driving full tilt up the side of a winding mountain road, I'd barely gone through any gas. Around me, the terrain changed, which was evident even through the limited light. The forest crawled closer to the road, the trees grew thicker and taller. Through the ascent, the road had narrowed, the shoulders almost non-existent, and the hills on either side were steeper. The longer I'd gone, the closer to losing control of the car I felt. Each corner seemingly arrived faster. I'd brake hard, the car always on the cusp of flipping into the ditch. The corners seemed sharper as well, which made me accelerate more at each straight stretch. I'd turned down the music, focused on the road, and cracked the sunroof to get some air circulating. With each corner that scared me, I questioned if I should pull over, knowing I shouldn't drive so erratically when I was this tired. If someone had offered me a pill to stay awake, I would've swallowed them by the handful.

Fighting through another sharp corner, a glint of light reflected from the side of the road. I slowed and pulled onto the shoulder as close as I could. I was weary of traffic coming from either direction, but the truth was, I hadn't seen another car since I'd turned right, and the chances of a vehicle appearing now were slim to none. Once stopped, I saw that the reflection was from a discarded sign in the ditch, partially covered by debris. A weird feeling came over me while I sat in the car, the engine idling. This felt strange, the entire situation, and I kept the engine running in case I needed to make a quick getaway. Undoing the seatbelt, I opened the door and stepped out. Having been in that car for almost eight hours, my knees ached as I stood. My lower back and hips welcomed the stretch as I pushed my hands high above me. A welcoming warmth caressed my body as I twisted and leaned back, feeling the muscles lengthen and relax. *Getting the blood flowing,* was what my dad used to call this. Even after that, I still hobbled over to the sign as though I was far older. Climbing down into the ditch, I used my shoe to kick the deadfall off. A big dent on one side of the sign caught my attention. The corner was crumpled, something hitting it so hard that even the paint was chipped, exposing the grey metal behind. Some of the reflective lettering was still visible, though faded. Kneeling, I wiped as much of the dirt away with my forearm as I could, allowing me to read what was exposed. *You'll never make it,* a deep voice said, causing me to stand and look around. The voice had been so loud and distinct that I could've sworn somebody was there. Nobody was. Confident I was alone; I returned my attention to the sign. The top line read: B - - ST BASIN .5. I couldn't read it all, as the dirt was so thick. The second line read: SUMMIT 2. The third read FUEL 50, and the bottom read EDGEWATER 250. I was close to the top. A place to rest. The fuel distance marker was self-explanatory. The other two lines made me nervous, but the line with the missing letters worried me more. Then something in the air *shifted.* It was subtle at first; the hairs on my neck raised, my ears twitched, and a cold sensation danced down my spine. *I'm not alone.* I looked again, expecting to find someone not far away, most likely the person who'd spoken before, but there was nobody around. Then the forest replied, a tree snapping loudly from within its depth. *The wind probably caused that.* I tried to convince myself that it wasn't anything to be concerned with. Then, I realized how quiet everything was. The sounds of nature – birds, wind, water and so on – had ceased. It was as though the mountain itself and all its inhabitants were collectively holding their breath, armed with the knowledge that something horrible was about to happen.

Within the trees, movement.

A shadow attached to something immense.

I should've run, but my feet wouldn't budge. Whatever that thing was, it filled the air with a toxic energy, a crackling sensation that suggested it was not happy with my presence.

SNAP!

The sound of another tree breaking rattled me. Then, from not far away, came the sound of a massive animal breathing hard. From between the trees I could see the air exhale, the coldness of the morning making the breath visible. From just above the exhales, two slivers of white. The beasts' eyes stared into my own.

A heartbeat later and an explosion of movement erupted from the darkness.

Whatever had been so still now rampaged towards me. I didn't move, frozen by the understanding I was going to die. I knew I couldn't outrun a bear, and whatever this was dwarfed that predator. As though I was moving in slow-motion, I forced myself to clamber from the ditch and run to the car, even as loud footfalls pounded the earth, getting closer behind me. Then, I was at the car. I yanked open the door and threw myself in, slamming it behind me, engaging the locks, and releasing the e-brake in one fluid sequence. I jammed the transmission into drive and gunned it, the gas pedal hitting the floor.

The car jolted forward, leaving the sign and whatever that creature was behind me. I raced down the road and over the next hill, before I had to slam the brakes, a tight right turn having appeared out of nowhere. Too focused on the road, I'd not yet looked behind me. Around the next turn, a slight descent greeted me, which knocked some of the tension in my neck down a notch. I reduced the pressure on the gas pedal, allowing the car to naturally slow while I tried to get my breathing under control. Another turn followed by another straight stretch, and after I'd directed the car over a small hump, suddenly I'd arrived at a basin. Sheer bluffs surrounded three sides of the span, the fourth open with a slight ascent that carried further away. The peaks of every side were snow-covered, while the colors of the hills below cascaded from dark green, to orange and lastly to brown. The road travelled from one side of the basin to the other and disappeared through an opening on the far side.

Shallow ponds, dotted with green growth across the surface edged up to the road. As I looked around the area, I noticed the trees had stopped along the bluffs, dense bushes and shrubs growing instead across the flats. At this elevation there were still two feet of snow on the ground, but the leafless branches of the shrubs pushed through the whiteness. As those branches somehow reminded me of the incident at the side of the road, my mind went back.

What the fuck was that creature? Probably just a deer.

I nervously laughed, my brain not believing the lie. *But still…* The rearview mirror confirmed nothing was behind me, and I laughed again at the absurdity of the situation. And damn, did it feel good to laugh. My shoulders relaxed more, even though I sounded exhausted.

At the speed the car was driving at, it crossed the basin in no time at all, and I was happy to have more miles between me and whatever that thing was. The road weaved higher, leaving the low of the basin, but reintroducing the terrain to further snowfall and slick road conditions. Nearing the apex, the tree-line thinned. With the distance between the clouds and the mountain top rapidly decreasing, I knew the summit would be upon me at any moment. A sign indicated a pullout was ahead in two kilometers. As it came into view, I slowed, flipped on the signal light, and left the road. Here, the snow was falling heavily, which greatly reduced visibility. Leaving the road was a relief, as above, the clouds were circling. A storm was brewing, and I didn't want to be on the road when it hit.

The lot had been plowed, but not recently, as an inch of snow covered the cement. Seeing the depth of snow on the other side of the barricades suggested it'd been snowing for some time this high up. A large mound of snow sat at one end of the lot, where the loader would dump it after plowing, but judging by the lack of any recent tracks, I knew it'd been a few days since anyone had even pulled into here. I parked near the wooden railing that separated the lot from where the washroom building was. It was a short span of land that would've been a wonderful place for a picnic during the sunny, summer months. On the far side sat the washrooms, a sign posted near the path stated that it had paid showers from June 1st until September 30th. It'd been hours since I'd last stopped to empty my bladder, and once I shut the car off the sudden urge to go hit. With the snow falling, I didn't want to leave the warmth of the car, but at least I'd be moving around. The inevitable stiffness from sitting so long was making my back ache. Opening the door, I stepped out and was immediately knocked back by a brutally cold wind. While the wind was relentless, the air was magical. I breathed in it, deeply, relishing the taste and how refreshing it was. Pure. It was far different from the polluted air I was used to breathing. I reached into the car, grabbed my jacket from the back seat, and slipped it on. It was too thin to really dampen the cold, but it did reduce the bite of the wind against my arms. I stretched, arms high, then pushed my hands deep into the pockets as I sauntered up the path to the washrooms. I was cautious about what would wait for me on the inside. Rest stops on the top of mountains weren't known to be the cleanest of places, and I expected the harsh aroma of stale piss and unflushed toilets to assault me as soon as I cracked the door open an inch. To my surprise, it was very clean and warm, the baseboard heaters humming as they kept the cold at bay. *Nice*, I thought. *At least I won't freeze my ass off.* I approached the urinal, unzipped, and proceeded to have the longest piss of my life. But the length of time standing there also began to work against me, and as I stood with my back to the door, I started to feel creeped out, and cursed myself for not choosing a stall. The hum of the baseboards harmonized with the wind outside, which didn't do anything to diminish the feeling that at any moment someone was going to burst into the washroom and attack while my defenses were down. Once finished, I washed my hands, doing all I could to not look in the mirror. I didn't want to see what I looked like. The reflection wouldn't be the me I remembered. I kept my hands under the water for as long as I could, enjoying the sting of the heat before I turned off the taps and grabbed some paper towels from the dispenser. All these little movements felt foreign, as though this was the first time I'd ever done any of this. My body was mine, but the movements seemed to be controlled from somewhere else. Still not looking at the mirror, I balled-up the towel and threw it towards the trash bin as though I was a professional basketball player, and after it hit dead center, I turned my focus towards the blast of cold air that would hit me when I went back out.

As expected, it did just that. I opened the door a crack and the wind howled, forcing me to leave before I risked getting slammed by the heavy door. Once outside, I felt exposed, and the feeling of being watched pressed down on me like a ten-ton weight. I jogged to the car, doing my best not to slip in the fresh snow. Even though it was only fifty feet away, the jog to the car felt good, my legs enjoying the movement. They wouldn't be happy when I was cramped behind the wheel soon enough. It was my focus on not falling that prevented me from looking at the car as I went, not until I'd made it back. Once there, I was stumped. How long had I been in there?

The car was covered in four inches of snow. The roof and hood were blanketed, so much so that I had to use my sleeve to wipe the snow away, just to be able to open the door. The cracking of branches in the trees and of the wind whipping through the forest made me feel even more exposed, making me desperate to get back in the car. I wanted to get out of this cold and hide from the world around me. The vastness of nature loomed around the parking lot, the wind creating a clattering of leaves that sounded like a small army of skeletons approaching. Far off in the distance a faint sound came to me, just under the leaves, one that had me perk up.

BEEP-BEEP-BEEP.

Beeping? It couldn't be, could it? What would be beeping way out here in the middle of nowhere? As I listened for it again, a sudden exhaustion slid over me, like someone had draped a weighted blanket over my shoulders. I was drained. It was a culmination of everything. The last few months of arguments. The appointments and phone calls discussing options. Yelling. So much yelling. No matter how the conversation would start, it would twist around towards what was going on and then we'd yell. And the crying. So much crying. Nobody understood. And when I'd try to explain, they'd cry.

With the exhaustion hammering me and the constant snowfall, I really had two options. The first would be to keep driving in the hopes that I'd come across a motel, where I could stop and get a room for the night. I'd sleep for two or three days. Maybe there'd be a room where that sign had indicated fuel. Or I could just sleep in the car, leave it running with the heat cranked and curl up on the back seat. The truth, though, was that I didn't have the energy to stay awake, let alone drive more. My body needed sleep, and there was a chance that the next place might even have a room. I'd be risking a drive through a snowstorm with the hope I'd not be sleeping in a parking lot of a gas station when there was a perfectly good place to sleep right here. And bonus – heated washrooms.

Decision made.

Crawling into the back, I grabbed the spare blanket from behind the passenger seat and wrapped it around me. I could hear *Her* voice in my head, *"See, I told you to always have an emergency blanket,"* which brought a smile to my face. Wiggling into position, I found it funny that I'd probably slept on this backseat a dozen times over the last few months.

So many arguments.

At least this time I wasn't going to sleep angry, I thought, and as sleep washed over me, I remembered I hadn't turned the heat on in the car. *Oh well*, I thought, *it shouldn't get that cold*. Instead, I fished the keys from my pocket, pressed the lock button, and heard the magnetic click of both doors locking, followed by the honk of the alarm.

I was asleep in moments.

*

Hours later, the sun wrestled me awake.

Rolling over, I propped myself up on one elbow and yawned, remembering where I was. It was cold in the car, but thankfully not freezing. The blanket had done its job. As soon as I shed it, I shivered, wrapping myself up again. As I sat there, getting my bearings, the peripheral images of a dream danced around in my head, but I couldn't get them to fully form. It'd been one of those dreams where I'd even told myself to not forget it when I woke, but the fog of waking up prevented me from piecing it together. All that remained were bright lights and a strange white hat, which didn't make sense. Not wanting to linger further, I unlocked the car and climbed out. I was glad to see the snow had stopped during the night, the amount on the hood and roof close to the same depth as when I'd gotten in the car. Standing there, my body ached, so I shook my arms, wiggled my legs, and did whatever I could to get the pins-and-needles that had developed because of jamming my six-foot frame into the four feet of space that the back seat offered. It was then that the sensation of being watched returned. Looking around, there were no other cars, nor were there tire tracks in the snow. The highway was unplowed, and I knew that if a plow truck had come by while I slept, surely, I would've heard it, but being as exhausted as I'd been, it wasn't out of the realm of possibility that I would've kept sleeping. But the sensation lingered, increased actually, when I looked across the highway, which did nothing to quell the anxiety that was growing. Deciding I should try and use the washroom once more before leaving, I closed the car door, but then paused. It was only then that the dozens of massive footprints in the snow, around the back of the car caught my attention. The snow was deep enough that each track was visible and defined. Stepping away from the car to examine them closer, my eyes were drawn to the set of footprints that led to the back of the car. I could follow them from the far side of the lot into the trees. *Was this the creature from before?* My blood ran cold when I rounded the car and saw the tracks stop at the back window. On the back window, I could make out the smudged facial features of something that'd looked inside.

Whatever that thing was, it'd been watching me while I slept and as I stood there, running this through my head, my bladder let go and I pissed myself.

6.

Disoriented and panicked, I came to, the last remnants of the feverish dream torn from my mind like a Band-Aid pulled while I wasn't looking. I could remember bits of it, the cold, the wind, the idea of being watched, but that was it. As the last strains of the dream faded away, and other things took their position in my brain, things that I simply didn't have an answer to. Like why was I so sore? Why did it feel like a monster truck had driven over me? And where the hell was I?

The Lighthouse.

Of course.

The strange building that seemed to be made from every Rorschach test ever made.

THUMP!

From above, the bane of my existence sounded, and as I turned my head to look, an excruciating pain ripped through my body. I clutched my left arm tight to my body, but as I did so, the brightness of the room forced my eyes shut. *Had it always been so bright?* Delicately, I tried to raise my arm, and was pleased to see that I could, but only to a point. After that, it hurt like hell.

Lifting it slowly a second time in a desire to see how far I could move it pain free, I noticed my wrist and caught my breath. It was alarmingly swollen. I'd twisted my ankle many years ago and it had ballooned, but even that was nothing compared to what was happening right now from my elbow down. A ridiculous thought crossed my mind as I looked at it, wondering if there was an x-ray machine somewhere within the building. And then I realized that even if there was, how would I operate it myself? I would've laughed at the absurdity of that thought if it wasn't for the fact that my arm throbbed, the pain flared, and I had to battle the urge to vomit against the sudden spinning of the room.

As the room slowed and my bearings returned, I decided to stand, hoping that my legs wouldn't fail me.

The edge of the couch seemed to be a mile away, even though I could see it was only inches. It took me a minute, but I managed to get to a sitting position, then waited for my legs to respond. I figured if I made sure they weren't tingling before I stood, they could be trusted, but I wanted the coffee table that sat just beyond my feet as leverage, just in case.

Wait... coffee table?

Had there been one before? I was positive there hadn't. *Maybe I just didn't see it?*

Either way, I knew I couldn't trust this place, so I returned my focus to the task of simply standing. The fact that the thought of attempting to do that even filled me with anxiety spoke volumes. Something that was normally so natural was now one of my biggest fears. Or, more accurately, the fear of getting to my feet and taking a tumble scared me most of all.

Taking a steadying breath, I wrapped my fingers around the edge of the couch. I told myself that I'd count to three and then rock my body forward, using momentum to help me up. Either my legs would work, or I'd fall flat on my face. I wanted to believe that wouldn't happen, but the prospect kept poking itself through my thoughts, no matter how positive I was trying to be.

Just shut up and go.

I counted.

One, two, three.

Rocking backwards half-an-inch, I then rocked forward and pushed with my legs and voila, I was on my feet. I hadn't even had to use the coffee table. Looking down at the couch, I saw the cushions were faded and worn. The longer I stared, the older they became, until I shook my head, and they appeared as I remembered them, new and unused. Taking a step, I stopped.

Something was different. Everything was different.

My arm no longer hurt. And stranger still, the swelling was gone. I flexed my hand, marvelling that I could see the knuckles move, and when I twisted my wrist around, the muscles in my forearms became defined and flexed, something impossible to see just moments ago when my arm was as big as a sack of potatoes. Stamping my feet, my legs felt solid, *and* I could feel both legs equally. What was going on? This was unexpected. I took another skeptical step. My balance didn't waiver. Two more steps. My legs responded, and with each additional step there was less and less pain throughout my body. Should I risk it and take advantage of this and race up the stairs? And if so, was I going up to try and find the source of the noise or to rip apart the kitchen in an attempt to quench my thirst?

But then I thought that maybe the Lighthouse was toying with me. It was wanting me to grow confident, and as soon as I took the bait and began to ascend – *BAM!* – it would pounce and down I'd go again.

Wanting to test my theory, which was suspect at best, I crossed the room twice, growing more and more emboldened with each step, and when another *THUMP* sounded, I walked straight to the spiral staircase. But before I could bring myself to start up, my eyes found where my shin had slammed into the step, and the dried blood I'd left behind. *Had I really hit it that hard?* It didn't matter one way or another, the damage had been done, and that was in the past. I took the steps two at a time, putting that level behind me, my curiosity taking me higher and higher.

Once I was at the precipice of the next level, I slowed, not wanting to rush into a situation where suddenly I was face-to-face with whatever it was that was causing the annoying as shit thumping sound. Better to be safe than sorry. For all I knew, it could very well be a rabid animal.

Or worse.

In my haste to race towards the sound, I'd not realized just how high I'd climbed. Here I was, at the top level.

The bedroom.

One entire side of the space was filled by a massive bed, perhaps the largest I'd ever seen, and for a brief moment I contemplated jumping from where I stood onto the mattress, just because I could.

There were few other pieces of furniture here, the bed taking up almost the entirety of the floor. To the right of the bed sat a two-drawer dresser, which looked as though it was from a child's playset in comparison to the bed. The bed itself was positioned beside a pair of glass doors, which opened outwards. From where I stood, it looked like a short deck was outside the doors. The floor plan wasn't ideal, as to get to those doors, you'd need to cross over the bed. Ignoring my sense of societal norms, I shimmied over and went to the doors. The glass was dirty and smudged, but I could see through it just enough to find a wooden deck. The wood was considerably newer than the main structure of the Lighthouse, and brighter, less weather decayed, which suggested it had been added not long ago. On the other side of the room, closer to the stairs, was a door. I figured a washroom would reside behind it but judging from the constant surprises this place had delivered already, I wasn't positive. Going to the door, I had the idea that maybe the culprit behind the mysterious *thump* was hiding within. The handle turned when I tried it, which threw me off guard. I'd expected to find it locked. Maybe I'd set myself up for an ambush, as I was unprepared, completely defenseless, not to mention sore, slow, and beat up. The icing on the cake was the fact I didn't have a weapon to defend myself with.

As the door swung open, I jumped into a very poor attempt at a karate attack position, one leg up, both arms above my head, in what must've resembled the most ridiculous crane of all time.

If someone had been hiding in the bathroom, I might've gotten the upper hand when they'd burst into laughter at how stupid I looked. Thankfully, nobody was there, nor did it appear that anybody had been for some time. There were no towels. No toilet paper. The space was lit from the light seeping in from a small, opaque window. Truth be told, the washroom was nicer than I'd expected, especially considering it was in this Lighthouse. It was clean, and when I opened the cabinet above the sink, even the narrow shelves were bare, and looked as though they'd just been wiped clean.

Leaving the bathroom, I discovered another door; one I was certain hadn't been there only a minute ago. I approached with caution, though I guessed it would be a closet, but the location in the space made no sense. Not that *much* was making sense.

Before opening the small door, I begged myself not to repeat my ninja move, but before I made that promise, the handle had been twisted and I pulled. The door flung open, slammed against the wall, as if my hand had its lost grip on the handle. I hadn't used much force, but the door had taken off like a rocket. So much for stealth. Initially, the space looked empty, but as I looked within, I could see that something had been scrawled on the back wall.

Tired.

Join the club, I thought with a smirk as I closed the door and turned back to the room.

Even though this was my place of residence, I took off my shoes to cross the bed. It seemed the polite thing to do, and I still wanted to respect the space and treat it as though I owned it. I kicked the shoes off, scurried across the mattress, and went to the glass doors. They pushed open easy enough, and as they swung out, one of the most amazing views I'd ever seen in my life was revealed. Stepping onto the deck, I marveled at what lay before my eyes.

Whoever decided to put the deck there had been a genius. Though it was only a dozen feet across and maybe six feet deep, when I stood at the railing, I was almost able to see around the entire building. Only the section directly behind me was blocked, not that anyone would want to gaze longingly on a boring, empty field. The water far below shimmered, and the low, white-capped waves that cascaded against the rocky shoreline sprinkled the air with a mist I could smell even from up here. The mountainous hills on the far side of the bay edged up and rose, the snow-tops shining as the sun danced across their peaks.

As I breathed deeply and admired the scenery, I felt a familiar tingling somewhere deep in my brain. My eyes darted up, surprised to find a single black cloud racing across the clear blue sky. As the cloud approached the sun, the sky darkened and the temperature dropped considerably, the wind from the bay raking across my exposed skin.

I desperately wanted to remain on the deck, to just stand and enjoy the brief moment of normality compared to the craziness that'd been happening, but the wind increased in intensity, and without a jacket on, I was at its mercy. Turning to retreat inside, my left foot became a solid rock, and I lost all feeling in it. And without any feeling, I couldn't hold myself up. I stumbled and toppled forward, the all-to-real thought of flying over the railing and falling to a watery death flashing before my eyes. Instead, I managed to get my other foot down. I pivoted and flopped towards the open doors, hoping I'd somehow land on the mattress within. That hope was fleeting, as my body slammed into the frame. The impact forced a yell of pain and pushed my body into a spin. As I spun away from the open door, both legs gave out and I found myself falling backwards. Expecting to slam onto the hard floor, I was relieved when I did land on the mattress. It was still with enough force that the wind was momentarily knocked from my lungs, and I bounced, flipping onto my stomach.

Even as I gasped for breath, I was happy. I was inside. I hadn't gone over the railing, nor had I landed on the deck or the floor. All-in-all, I'd consider that a win.

Staying where I was, I took some deep breaths while getting my bearings. The feeling in my right leg had returned, which was a relief and frustrating in equal parts. Why'd my leg lock up on me? It still felt like a two-by-four attached to my body instead of any sort of appendage. I couldn't feel it, couldn't move it and if I had a saw, I very well might've hacked it free from my body. *Losing it here, buddy.* I tried shaking the leg, but to no avail. It simply wouldn't respond. I sat, as best I could, considering half of my lower body was useless, and started to punch my thigh, hoping the muscle would respond. When it didn't, I upped the force behind each punch, knowing that when the sensation returned – if it ever did – I'd be cursing myself over the bruise I was creating with each solid strike. It was while doing this that I caught a flash of movement out of the corner of my eye. It was barely perceptible, as though something had sped across the deck, momentarily blocking the sun from shining in through the open door.

Someone's out there.

Forcing my good leg to do the work, I hobbled from the bed and limped out, knowing I'd finally found who was making that noise. At this point, I didn't care if both legs gave way, as I'd fall forwards, and, if luck was on my side, I'd land on the person. Right as I made it to the opening, the doors swung shut, slamming with an audible bang, though not hard enough to break the glass. I stood in shock, wondering if it had been a gust of wind, when a deafening boom shook my eardrums, pushing me back from the doors. My ears rang, my head swam, but even in that state of disorientation, I heard through the muck the unmistakable sound that had pushed me to the edge of my sanity.

THUMP!

Directly above.

How was that possible?

And who'd been on the deck?

7.

Terrified.

The prints were in the snow and on the window.

I stared at them for what felt like hours, my brain racing through every scenario possible, but it didn't matter how off-the-rails my imagination went. The reality was that something had been watching me.

Something had been watching me.

It was tempting to place a hand or foot beside one for a size comparison, but I knew if I did that my brain would turn to mush, or rather, mushier than it was currently.

What could've made these? I couldn't think of a single animal that existed in the world that could've made these tracks. What if it was something unknown to science? I didn't think so. Even as I stared at the evidence directly in front of me, I simply couldn't bring myself to believe this was from something unknown. Snow began to fall again while I stood there, my piss-soaked pants hardening and threatening to freeze to my skin, so I grabbed a fresh pair of jeans and boxers from the bag in the car and trudged towards the washrooms through the ever-deepening snow. Halfway to the building, I stopped. Maybe my mind had been playing tricks on me. Maybe there were no tracks at all, and the brightness of the snow had messed with my eyes, exhaustion making me see something that wasn't actually there. I hustled back, but when my eyes found the tracks were still there, I sighed.

They were real.

Jesus.

Seeing them there, in front of me, snapped my brain into acceptance, and I briskly walked back to the washrooms. A part of me suggested I run, but another part said that if I *were* to run, that would just bring unwanted attention my way.

Once inside, I went directly into a stall and closed the door. Even though not a single car had passed by while I was there, I didn't want somebody to walk in while I was changing, finding me with my urine-covered pants around my ankles.

With the soiled pants and boxers off, my thighs and crotch were still damp and sticky. I'd pissed myself a few years back after getting hammered at a bar. I'd drank until I was stumbling around and had bumped into a busty redhead. Her drink had flown from her hand, splashing across the chest and face of a roided-up meathead. I was attempting a slurred apology to the Jessica Rabbit look alike, when a fist had slammed into my stomach and as I let out a loud 'oooooopphhhhh,' my bladder had let go, piss changing the front of my jeans from a faded blue to a dark circle. I can still remember the redhead laughing and pointing as I looked down and watched in horror as the dark stain spread down my inner thighs. My friends had dragged me from the bar before the DJ was alerted and the entirety of the bar patrons laughed at my expense.

This all came flooding back to me as I stood half naked in the stall, realizing I didn't have any towels to clean my legs off with. After my bar wetting, my friends had stripped me nude and tossed me in a shower, which had helped sober me up at the same time. I didn't have any of that. No friends. No shower. And worse, no towels. On tiptoes, I looked over the wall of the stall, finding I was still alone. I hadn't expected to see anyone, but I was still on edge. Rushing, I went to the nearest sink, cranked out some paper towels and ran them under the tap, before doing my best to wipe my inner thighs clean. *I shouldn't have stopped here*, I told myself as I wiped. I should've kept driving, continuing until I found a gas station or a hotel.

As I finished, my left leg was tingling, a result of the weird way I'd propped myself near the sink to clean myself off. I shook my leg, wanting the sensation to leave, but I forgot about it when I tossed the paper towel in the garbage. A sound caught my attention. Something was walking around the exterior of the building. With each *crunch-crunch-crunch* of steps, I could follow where it was behind the structure. *What the fuck is that?*

Scared, I darted back into the stall, hastily slipping my legs into the clean boxers and jeans. From how cold it had been, the jeans were stiff, as though I'd dried them in the sun, but I didn't care. It felt better to be in rigid clean jeans than the ones I'd pissed. I wasn't sure what I should do with them, so I opened the stall door a few inches, just enough to get my arm out, and underhanded them into the garbage. Then I closed the door and took a seat on the toilet, praying for whatever was outside to leave.

*

I wasn't sure how long I sat there, but after not hearing anything from outside in what felt like an hour, I decided it was time to go. Needing extra time to get some confidence, I counted to one hundred in my head, and, after still hearing nothing, left the stall and slowly approached the main door to the washrooms. In my mind I had this picture of a giant, hairy, humanoid creature with only one ear and two-foot-long fangs waiting just outside to devour me. I tried to tell myself that was absurd, but then my brain would reply with, '*Remember the tracks?*' If I could've smacked my brain to try and get it to shut up, I would've. Instead, I steeled my nerves and opened the door, waiting to see what awaited me.

As the door opened, the only thing to assault me was the blast of cold air and snow.

Is it snowing even harder? I thought. *The longer I'm here, the heavier the snow is.* It was time to get moving, to get away from this rest stop and these washrooms.

The walk towards the car was unnerving. I felt exposed, as though I was being paraded before things hiding in the trees, waiting to choose which one of the beasts would get to chomp on me first.

After a half dozen steps, I stopped. The hairs on the back of my neck stood up, and even through my jacket I could feel goose bumps forming across my arms.

Something had changed.

I was being watched.

I felt like now, more than ever, the sound of an approaching car would settle my nerves, but it was as though the road had been closed in either direction since the moment I'd made that dreaded turn.

As I focused on my surroundings, I was reminded of my brief stop at the discarded road sign. There were no sounds whatsoever. Not even the wind clattering through the trees or a crow cawing from high above. I wiped some of the heavy flakes from my eyebrows, licking my lips nervously, and took a step. The sound of my foot crunching through the snow echoed like a shotgun blast around me. I froze, my eyes darting in every direction. Nothing moved.

Daring myself to keep going, I tentatively approached the car, feeling more like a member of the bomb squad waiting to see if the device would explode than a dude who'd just pissed his pants. *Why did it feel like something had changed?* Nothing immediately stood out, nothing that was out of place or different. Certainly, the snow hadn't stopped falling.

A plow coming by would be nice, I thought, wondering just how dreadful the drive down the mountain would be. *And just how much farther could the car go?* I'd need gas sooner than later, but if it was slow going due to the weather, that would put a damper on things as well. I resigned myself to the very real thought that I'd need to walk to find gas at some point in the future. Which also reminded me that I didn't have a container or Jerry Can of any sort in the car, so I'd need to buy something to carry the gas back. It was all already sounding expensive and exhausting, and I hadn't even left the parking lot yet.

Lost in thought, my ears perked up when I heard something off to my left. At first it was like a big animal was breathing forcefully. I saw nothing, but much like at the road sign, I hadn't seen anything at first either. Another sound came, this time louder, more violent, as though a branch had been purposefully snapped in two.

I remained dead still.

Another huff out, off to the left. Closer. Louder.

CRUNCH.

Something large took a step, breaking through the heavy snow.

Run you fool.

Another two steps sounded, the ground vibrating below my feet. I was petrified, unable to move, my feet unwilling to do what my brain screamed so desperately for them to do.

RUN!

Something hurled past me – I wasn't sure what. It whizzed by and was swallowed by the snow – either a rock or a stick. I instinctively ducked as another object zipped by, the air crackling from the speed of the thing thrown.

Get in the car!

I stumbled towards the vehicle, the *thing* approaching faster and faster, and with each successive step, the ground shook, threatening to make me lose my footing and collapse in the snow.

At the car door, I struggled to grab the handle twice, my hand shaking, the snow making the handle slick. Finally, I squeezed the handle and pulled, but stopped when the back end of the car lifted from the ground, a deafening roar throwing me back from the vehicle.

I back-peddled through the snow, crab-walking for my life. I expected the car to sail into the air at any moment and crush me to a pulp. Instead, another roar erupted. The car was dropped, and when it did, the back window smashed. The bouncers blocked whatever had lifted the car from view, but I caught a brief glimpse of the top of a darkened head, just as it disappeared into the trees at the far end of the parking lot. I got to my feet, hands on my head in shock over what had just occurred. *Was the car destroyed? Could it still be driven?*

I circled around to the back to inspect the damage, only to find an already congealed splattering of blood. Within the middle of the red fluid remained two large footprints. From off in the distance another roar echoed.

This one felt like it was directed specifically at me.

8.

I've been a horror movie fan for as long as I can remember.

When I was younger, I couldn't wait until the weekend arrived. I'd lay in bed until I heard the house go quiet, doing my best to fake sleep until it was safe to sneak out to the living room. There, I'd position myself a few feet from the screen, wincing when I pulled the knob that turned the tv on, the old tube humming to life. I'd rapidly turn the dial of the volume down, making sure that it didn't suddenly blare noise into the stillness of the house. I would then slowly turn the dial – each click sounding like a rocket launch in the silence around me – until the channel I was searching for arrived. Broadcasting from out east, before every movie started, it aired a computer graphics display that had 80's synth music playing over it, as the graphics merged and shifted and morphed. I loved watching them, wishing they played them earlier in the day so I could crank the volume up and sing along to each song. When it faded out and the parental warning played, I was always giddy with excitement, unsure what would be coming on to watch. We didn't have a guide to read, or a button to push. No, I would sit cross-legged in the middle of our living room floor, waiting to see what craziness would air that night. Would it be a new movie? Or one I'd seen a dozen times already? Back then, I didn't care. All that mattered was that heads were decapitated, sometimes I'd get to see bare breasts, and crazy monsters and creatures would wreak havoc throughout whatever small town the film was set in. Low budget, B horror movies were my bread and butter, and I absolutely loved every single one that they aired.

If I was to try and put a number on how many horror movies I've watched between the impressionable age of eight and to the one I watched just a few short days ago, I'd say a conservative estimate would be around fifteen hundred.

So, what does this have to do with anything, you may ask? Well, you see, the number of decapitations, mutilations, and senseless violence I'd sat through on film over three decades, in no way, shape or form prepared me for what a large amount of blood looks like in person. I wasn't prepared for what it smelled like, and, most assuredly, I wasn't prepared for the pure shock of understanding just where it may have come from.

I don't know why I didn't vomit.

All I knew was that the thing lurking around was the reason for this blood. And *fuck* was it a lot of blood. *What if the crunching I was hearing was the sound of this thing eating its victims?* I was numb. I'd believed the noise was from this thing marching through the underbrush. But what if it was destroying bones with its teeth? The thought that this beast was eating everything that got in its way was the slap I needed to get moving.

I was next.

In a panic, and with the very real image of a huge pool of blood flooding my brain, I jumped into the car. I knew I needed to settle, to calm down and focus, or there'd be no chance the car would turn on. I'd muddle it and turn the keys and I'd be met with the laughter of an engine failing to turn over. Instead, something even worse happened when I reached for the keys.

My hand found nothing.

I scrambled, my fingers dancing around the ignition, searching for the keys, but there was nothing there. They simply weren't in the ignition.

For a split second I thought the beast had somehow managed to get in the car and steal them while my focus was elsewhere, but then it dawned on me.

I'd put the keys in my pocket last night before I climbed onto the back seat. It was the reason I hadn't turned the heat on. I'd just hit the fob to lock the doors. Remembering this crucial piece of information, I stuffed my hand frantically in my pocket, searching for the keys, but again found nothing.

And then again, I remembered the sequence of events that had played out.

The keys that were supposed to be in my jean pocket, were sitting discarded and covered in urine a hundred feet way in the garbage can in the bathroom. Looking through the windshield of the car, the bathroom building appeared to be in another time zone. As though I'd need to hike up Everest and then K2 after, just make it to the door.

An expectation of a sudden attack had me frantically looking out each side of the car, thankful that a monstrous face never once met my gaze back. With each direction clear, or as clear of a beast as I could tell, I knew now was the time to make the dash to the building. If I didn't go now, I'd never work up the courage to do so again.

Taking what felt like forever to pull the latch out and open the door, I held my breath, praying to a higher power – which one didn't matter – that the hinges wouldn't reply with their unoiled groan. I mentally chided myself while pushing the door further and further away from the frame of the car, as I'd meant to oil the hinges months ago, but never got around to it. Once it was wide enough that I felt comfortable I'd be able to slink free, I delicately put my left leg out, pausing when my foot planted on the ground. Nothing stirred. Shifting my weight, I used the frame itself as a point to grab and pull, and climbed free, stopping again when my right foot was on the ground. Was it safe to breathe? I wasn't positive it was, but at the same time knew it was a necessary thing to do if I wanted to remain upright.

Using the car as a ridiculously oversized shield, I surveyed the area again, knowing my brain needed just as much confirmation that nothing was waiting to pounce as my muscles did. Once satisfied that I was alone, I plotted my path and went for it, running faster than the fastest Olympic sprinter had ever run before.

How fast did I cover that distance? No idea. A radar gun might've exploded once it processed the speed I was travelling at, or – and this was the more likely scenario – a sad emoji face would've popped onscreen, the device ashamed of how slow I was moving in real time. None of that mattered though, as I zipped over the ground, believing whole-heartedly that I was going to make it to the bathroom building.

Reaching the door and grabbing the handle, I breathed a sigh of relief as I forced my way inside the warm interior, not caring that the door flung open with such force that it slammed against the outside wall. The warmth inside was heavenly, but I immediately froze, the sound of the door echoing around the open parking area. *I'm a dead man*, I thought, as I tip-toed back to the door and pushed it open an inch. Looking around the area, I was relieved to find it still empty. *Take it slow*, I told myself. *Don't make any stupid mistakes.*

As I started to close the door, a rustling to my right sounded, and my brain threw the absolute fucking worst thought I'd ever had directly into my mind.

What if it's invisible?

I should've laughed at the absurdity of it all, but I was so panicked over the possibility of being eviscerated that I just couldn't force even the smallest of chuckles.

Feeling like I was pushing my luck with how long I'd already been away from the car and the ever-hardening pool of blood, I darted to the garbage can, throwing my hands into it without a care over what else I might grab. My hands scrambled through damp paper towels, something that felt crusty, something that felt hard and squishy at the same time, and, finally, the dense wetness of my discarded jeans. *This is my chance to survive*, I thought, pulling them from the trash. Once they were out into the light of the washrooms again, I grimaced at the urine-drenched garment, knowing I'd need to fish through my accident to find the keys. I rushed to do it, flailing around with no hope to get them free, so I went to the counter near the sinks and set them down, laying them flat. Now with the pants flat, I grabbed the keys from the pocket, and tossed the jeans back in the garbage, hoping that would be the very last time I'd ever see them. Of course, in my haste to discard them, I threw them like I was making a basketball shot, and the wet, heavy jeans slammed into the bottom of the garbage bin, which hit the wall behind it, a clattering echo ricocheting throughout the small structure like a brass band had taken up residence.

Staying still, I heard no response from outside; no crunching of snow (or bones), and no sound of anything approaching. I was still in good shape.

It was while I remained at the door that I started to notice a few subtle 'issues' I was having. The first was that my feet were freezing cold. My shoes weren't designed for snow, or to keep anything warm. They were designed for people to run in, even if all I did was casually walk around in them. The second was that my hands were just as cold as my feet, my fingers numb, and not having any gloves on was making it worse by the second. It was at the moment I stretched my fingers, attempting to try and use my movement to warm them up, when my palms slid free of their perch and I toppled forward, my head smacking the frame of the door. I bounced back from the door, which I instinctively reached for, and while my left hand found the handle, my other flew out beside me, and I closed the door on the numb fingers of the right hand.

I stifled a yell, the pain rocketing throughout my hand. My fingers throbbed, so in an attempt to calm them, I shoved them in my pocket, where I found the key fob waiting for me and before I understood what was happening, my fingers connected with the button on the fob and, as my brain comprehended what was about to happen, heard the locks for the car click at the same time the lights flashed and the horn honked once, alarming the car.

Up until that moment, I'd thought I'd somehow ended up in the clear, that whatever caused that massive pool of blood behind the car had somehow forgotten about my existence and moved on to greener pastures.

But with the alarming of the car, that potential was squashed almost immediately, as not far away the crack of branches sounded and something large began making its way towards me, this thing not caring in the least about the chaotic noises it made as it stomped through the trees.

Before I could let my fear take hold and prevent me from moving, I took off in a full sprint, leaving the warmth of the bathrooms behind me. I didn't look anywhere else but directly at the car, and no matter how frozen, numb or painful my hand was, I wasn't going to let go of those keys ever again.

I knew that if I didn't make it to the car, I'd be dead and judging by how close whatever it was that was hunting me down was getting, I didn't have much time left to live.

9.

During my teen years, I went through a time where I just didn't want to be alive. I lost the desire to deal with the boredom and tedious aspects that life presented. The feeling that I was living my very own Groundhog Day just didn't appeal to me. Wake up. Eat. School. Homework. Eat. Sleep. Repeat. Monotony wasn't something I was interested in experiencing five days a week. But man did I relish the weekends.

Sports.

Reading, music, hunting, all those things really turned my crank. For the most part, I made a decent effort to wade through the hell that was my week, in order to enjoy the weekends.

Then that changed.

I had a moment of clarity on a long walk one night.

I'd been going on longer walks each night when insomnia had taken hold, not wishing to sit awake while the rest of the house snored away. Like most of those walks, on this one I was hoping beyond hope that a wild animal would savagely attack me and end everything. It was my cowardly way of hoping something else would finish me off because I hadn't worked up the nerve to do it myself. But on this particular walk, with the moon shining down and the stars dancing above, I realized that if I truly cared so little about myself, why should I let some animal do it? It was time for me to step up and deal with it on my own. So, I walked to a bridge, in the middle of the long straight stretch down the highway and climbed over the railing.

Standing on the edge of the bridge, with my back pressed firmly against the metal railing, I looked up at that bright moon and gave it a smile while tears streamed down my face.

Then, I jumped.

There was a brief moment, during free fall, where I felt at peace, a calmness washing over me. That all the hurt and sadness would be over, and whatever came next would simply... come. But, in this case, it wasn't to be. I'd made a criminal stupid mistake. I should've looked before I leaped.

Instead of falling the fifty feet or so that I expected, to land hopefully headfirst on the sharp and twisted rocks below, I dropped a staggeringly miniscule three feet, hitting the side of the grassy bank away from the rocks, and rolled away in pain as I twisted my ankle.

I struggled to my feet and worked my way up the short bank, pulling myself over the concrete barricade before I sat and shook my head. The annoyance of limping all the way home stung, and I kept thinking about just how much of a loser I was that I'd failed that attempt so feebly.

The embarrassment didn't subdue more attempts to leave this mortal plane. Over the next few months, my thoughts turned darker, and, after some outward displays of not caring if I lived, I was admitted to the small, local hospital for observation.

On one particular evening, my friends had come by, as had my family. After they'd left, only my dad remained. I'd had a relationship of convenience with my dad, one that I'd elevated to a status it had never truly been, but had always been based around his interests and allowing me to tag along. When he went golfing, I went golfing. When he went hunting, I went hunting, and so on. I knew he wanted to practice his shooting for old timers' hockey, so I'd play in goal, pretending to be

Patrick Roy while he snapped shot after shot at me. It was my way of connecting with him because we wouldn't otherwise.

That evening, I saw his eyes were misty with tears, something I'd never seen before. As he gave me a hug, he said, 'Get better, bud. We're all very worried about you.' He left before I could offer a reply. I tried to process what he'd said. I wanted to believe he'd meant it, but based on how things usually were between us, I took it with a grain of salt. But, the phrase he'd said… it resonated. It had been something I'd heard from the few friends I still had over and over. I needed to make a change, and needed to figure out a way to keep going, a desire to stay alive.

You may be asking yourself why I share this brief interlude.

Well, because people always say things like, 'My life flashed before my eyes.' And, when you're 100% positive that your life is about to end, it seemed that this random flicker of a moment was what decided to fly through my brain as I ran towards the car, the immense death-beast barreling towards me.

No matter how fast I felt like I was running, the blurred shape of the massive, giant beast crashing through the trees and growing closer seemed to be moving faster than me.

With my legs pumping, I should've covered that span in three seconds flat, but instead, it was as though I was moving in slow motion. I could see each and every snowflake form in the air before my eyes as it fluttered to its death on the ground below. I'd been confident I'd get to the car and zip away before the brute bashed my brains in, but the ever-growing concern that this thing was controlling time and had somehow slowed me and sped itself up seemed to be the only possible explanation. No matter how hard I ran, it was like I was running in molasses. As I screamed inside my head, a second memory flashed within my brain.

This time, I was transported back to the veterinarian's office, on the day that my dog, Jake, passed away.

A small mixed terrier breed, Jake had been my loyal companion for close to a decade. Pushing the scales at maybe twenty pounds, he was a snuggle bug with me, but had a vicious bark and no problem snapping at people if their hands got too close to his mouth.

One day, we noticed lumps had grown all over his little body. The lumps were very painful, not only when you accidentally touched one while petting him, but also when he sat or laid on one. After discussing the best course of action, we decided it wasn't fair for him to suffer.

So, the dreaded appointment was made with the vet.

As much as I didn't want him to leave us, I knew this was the only way to end his suffering. Once in the room, the atmosphere was heavy, the veterinary technician kind. My mom was hysterical. I didn't know if it was real or performative, but either way, she wasn't able to stay in the room. She left to sit in the waiting room. I was only sixteen, too young to deal with this alone, but I knew I had to be there for him, just like he'd been there for me over the years.

Even within the operating room, we could hear my mom sobbing from next door, but because of my age, I did my best to stay stoic, some ridiculous internal machismo telling me I couldn't cry in front of these strangers. The vet came in and said a few words that the hum of blood coursing through my ears prevented me from hearing. I finally let the tears fall as they inserted a syringe into Jake's thin forelimb and the vet told me that a warm, soothing sensation would wash over him. The vet tech explained that for Jake, it would just seem like he was going to sleep, but in this case it was forever. They suggested that I pet him, that my stroke's would feel familiar and calming and my comfort would help him as the medication did its job.

At first, I was hesitant to touch him, not wanting to cause him any pain by hitting any of the lumps, but then I reached over and let my hand comb his short hair, the tears coming faster and thicker. As he laid on the steel table, he turned his little snout towards me, as though even through the thickness of the medication, he knew it was me, and licked my hand. I leaned down and kissed the side of his furry face, continuing to stroke him from head to tail. His breathing began to slow. His eyes glazed over and then shut. And his limbs stretched out, the muscles relaxing and his body slackening. I felt him push back against my hand, really enjoying the last few pets he would ever receive.

Good boy, I heard myself saying, in between sobs. *You were a good boy, Jake.*

I leaned in again, whispering how much I loved him and that I'd keep him in my heart forever.

And that was it.

The best friend I'd ever had and my most reliable confidant stopped breathing.

We'd brought a blanket from home, one that he'd loved, so we wrapped him in that, and I carried him out to the minivan. I set this tiny package down, in the back, this thing that used to be Jake, and closed the back door. Then we drove home, not a word spoken.

My sisters were already crying as we pulled into the driveway, but I ignored them and grabbed the blanketed bundle from the back. I carried him through the back of our property, to the base of the mountain that butted up to the edge of the trees, and we buried him there, still wrapped in the blanket.

As the memory played through my brain, I struggled to make sense of the '*why.*' Why this? Why now? The only think I could fathom was that it was an emotional kick in the ass from Jake, somewhere from the beyond, telling me I better fucking make it to that car, or all those moments we shared together were meaningless.

And, as though it was a direct response to the memory, my legs seemed to break free of the molasses that had grabbed hold so firmly, and I was flying over the path, my feet barely hitting the cement. When I was only a dozen feet from the car, I rapidly hit the unlock button, knowing that time was of the essence. I heard the locks pop, the lights flashed, and I ran to the driver side door. I frantically grabbed the handle, desperately wanting to get inside. While doing this, I begged myself not to look over, not to look towards whatever it was that was chasing me, but I knew it was a battle I was going to lose.

And then I looked.

What greeted me could only be described as an abomination.

Something birthed from the depths of hell, a beast so hideous that to look upon it for any length of time would've made a person go insane.

Understanding that this thing rampaging towards me only had red in its eyes, I jumped into the driver's seat and shoved the key into the ignition. As the car turned on, I slammed the door shut, threw the car into reverse, and backed up over the giant blood patch. I grabbed the shifter, slipped it into drive, and gunned it, my foot hitting the gas pedal so hard that I was surprised it didn't go straight through the floor of the car. Within the blood and the snow, the tires spun for a brief moment, long enough for me to notice, before they gained traction and the car shot forward. I raced from the parking lot, away from the horror that had almost crushed me. I didn't look back, instead keeping my focus on the road in front, knowing full well that if I crashed now, the beast would be on me in no time.

I never looked back, but that didn't mean that as I rounded the corner and the pullout disappeared from view, I didn't hear the roar of anger the beast let loose. It was delivered with such fury that even a half mile away it made the hairs stand up on my arms.

As I raced away, safe for the moment, I smugly believed that I'd left the beast far behind me, in the past.

I've never been more wrong in my life.

10.

THUMP.

Seriously, what the fuck was making that noise?

I sat, putting my shoes back on, trying to make sense of what had just happened, when the noise returned. *What had that been?* I was filled with more questions than answers, more uncertainty over what was going on. Had it just been a cloud? Or was it some giant bird that had crashed into the side of the Lighthouse?

That didn't seem right. If a large bird was flying at a high rate of speed and struck the Lighthouse, surely it would've broken something, or even fallen to the deck. And if it had done that, it would've hit me. Regardless, I needed to continue my search for the source of that noise. Before I went up, I wanted something to drink. I was suddenly so thirsty, my mouth dry and my tongue heavy, that I realized I couldn't remember the last time I had drank anything. *When was the last time I ate?* Thinking back to when I'd been at the kitchen level, I didn't remember there being anything in the fridge. The cupboards had been bare, not even any plates or glasses. I was pretty sure I still had some water, but that was all the way down at the bottom of this place. *I'd bought it at that gas station*, I thought, though that had felt like a million years ago already.

Did I leave the water bottle in the car? Or was it in my backpack down by the main door? Everything was foggy, especially when I tried to think specifically about when I'd arrived. Either way, the reality was that the bottle of water was all the way at the bottom of the Lighthouse, which meant I'd need to take the stairs down to retrieve it. *Why couldn't this place have an elevator?*

Standing, I paused to make sure my legs felt ok, not wanting a repeat of my prior episodes. While doing that, I examined what I could see of the deck again, making sure that nothing was looking back at me. Once confident that there hadn't been a giant bird, and that my legs were going to cooperate, I went to the stairs and began the tentative journey down. I simply couldn't bring myself to trust my legs, my confidence in them doing their job having eroded.

Descending, I arrived at the landing with the couch and table. The coffee mug was still there, which seemed to create a static feeling in the air. It compelled me to look at the calendar, but by doing so, it instantly had me confused. I could've sworn the calendar had a different date previously. The current date it displayed was July 1981, and, as well, there was no writing on the dates below.

I went to the table, examining the calendar closely. The image for that month was at first unnoticeable, until I realized it was an image of this very lighthouse. I let my eyes linger over the building. It didn't say when the photo was taken, but I could see the deck that jutted out from the bedroom level. Upon the deck was a small child, wearing a bright red jacket. They were holding two balloons in one hand, while they pointed out towards the bay with the other. The Lighthouse had its huge light focused on the water, right near a ship that was passing through the bay. I couldn't make out the name of the ship upon the side of the vessel, but seeing the faded name across the side of the boat filled me with a sense of déjà vu. *Had something like this happened before?* With nothing else of note in the image, I continued my search for water, happy that my left side seemed to be feeling better, almost trustable. *Maybe I won't bruise too badly?*

Arriving at the kitchen level, I decided to double check the fridge, hoping that maybe I'd missed something the first time around. Had I looked in the fridge? I didn't think so, but it already felt like it had been days since I was last here, so I wanted to see for myself. If I didn't and found water in here later, I'd curse myself to the ends of the world and back.

I pulled the door to the fridge open, and after the light had popped on, I wasn't surprised to find the inside empty.

Getting groceries would be a top priority. That was, after I figured out what in hell was making that sound.

I turned my focus to the cupboards that lined the wall, hoping maybe to luck out and find a bottle of water or something in them. Opening every door, I only found a few cups. One had words printed on the side that read whoever drank from that cup, would in fact be the #1 Dad of All Time! *Wow, such high expectations,* I thought, with a smirk. On the wall beside the cupboards was a small 4" x 4" drawing I hadn't noticed previously. The drawing was of Earth. Around the Earth emanated squiggly lines, with a caption that read; *"What if the whole world farted at the same time?!"*

I burst out laughing.

I couldn't contain it.

I was laughing as hard, if not harder, than I'd ever laughed before.

Tears were rolling down my face as I snorted and breathed in jerky gasps.

I would've kept laughing if my eyes hadn't found the picture on the wall again, and another strong sense of déjà vu washed over me. *Had I seen that photo before somewhere?* I couldn't place it, but I was positive I'd seen it before, and positive it hadn't been upon my first visit to this level of the Lighthouse.

After staring at it far too long, I shook my head one last time and took the stairs to the main level, finding my backpack sitting on the short bench near the front entrance. Feeling mentally and physically drained from the voyage up and down the Lighthouse stairs, I slumped onto the bench, mentally thanking whoever had put this here in the first place. Not only was it an efficient place to put your shoes on, but it was far more comfortable than a wooden bench had any right to be. Sitting there, I looked over at my backpack, just an arms length away. It felt more like it was a mile away. I summoned the energy to lift my arm, holding my hand out towards it, and focused all my telekinetic powers on the bag, begging for it to fly through the air so that I could grab it. Of course, I didn't have telekinetic powers, nor was a Jedi of any sense of the word, so that bag remained where it sat and I let my hand drop, dejectedly reaching over and grabbing it. Right away it felt too light to be concealing the big bottle of water that I'd believed to be inside. Unzipping the bag, I grabbed out the bottle that *was* inside and pulled it free. Fuck. There was less than a mouthful remaining in the bottom, and with my luck it'd be warm as piss. I untwisted the cap, brought the bottle to my lips, and tipped it. I knew before the small amount of water entered my mouth that it was going to be warm, judging by the heat radiating off the plastic that had connected with my lips. I swirled it around once before swallowing it down. I went to toss the bottle in annoyance into the corner, but then stopped, knowing the bottle might come in handy again in the future.

Did I have another bottle in the car? I was fairly certain I did. Usually, gas stations were trying their best to have you spend more in a single transaction by upselling to the customer with buy one for five bucks or buy two for seven-fifty. Sure, the second one *was* a deal, but you were still paying more per transaction. I wasn't sure why I was going off on this internal rant about upselling to myself, but I paused my train of thought to decide my next move. Go back up and fill the bottle with water using the tap at the sink or go outside and see if there was a bottle of water in the car.

Looking back up the stairs, I decided it was closer to the car and I figured I might as well take a look and see if I had anything else stashed there.

It wasn't until I was at the door and gave it a pull that I remembered how hard it'd been to open the first time. *Had I even fully closed it after?* I thought so, but wasn't positive. Either way, it was closed now, and I wondered if I could even muster enough energy to force it open.

I grasped the handle again and pulled, digging my heels into the floor as hard as I could. It didn't matter. I couldn't shift the door even an inch. I sat again, the bench as comfortable as ever, and examined the door. There had to be a way to open it, but how? Also, why was it stuck so firmly? Surely, if a Lighthouse was to be operated, the entrance into the place should be working?

My frustration growing, I went to the door, grabbed the handle, and jerked it back and forth, hoping my sudden movement would unstick whatever the fuck was stuck and somehow dislodge the door.

Nothing.

It was solidly shut.

"Fuck!" I bellowed, my voice echoing up and up towards the very top of the Lighthouse. *Maybe my shout would bring the noise-causer down to investigate, save me any more hassle,* I thought.

When nothing replied, and the very appearance of the door in my field of vision began to piss me off, I decided to see if I could get a window open and climb through. There was a round window halfway up the first set of stairs, so I turned my attention to that, trying not to lose my cool over the whole situation.

I begrudgingly trudged up the stairs, more a petulant toddler than man, and stopped at the steps near the window. To my dismay, the exterior of the window appeared to be blocked. Something in front of it prevented me from seeing out. How the hell was that possible? There weren't any trees outside, nor buildings. Par for the course, I figured. Everything revolving around this stupid Lighthouse was messed up, and nothing made any sense.

BANG!

A noise from far above rattled everything, including the glass within the frame of the window.

"Oh, shut up already!" I hollered back at whatever was causing the sound, not caring anymore if it was a blood-thirsty killer or not. I just wanted to fucking go outside and see if my fucking bottle of water was in the fucking car where I might've fucking left it.

Use this anger, I heard myself whisper inside my head. *Go, open the door.*

I was right. In my ever-spiraling state of craziness, I decided to listen to myself and stomped back over to the door, grabbed the handle, and pulled as hard as I could.

For one second, I laughed like a madman. Then, when the door didn't shift, I let go and wound up to punch the wall, deciding to really let my frustrations fly. I stopped when I noticed a light shining on the wall.

It couldn't be...

I turned and saw that it was what it seemed to be.

Daylight from outside was shining in through the window. The window that had just been completely blocked by some odd thing on the exterior.

I jogged up the stairs to look out, to see if I could climb through, but instead I was completely thrown for a loop once again.

The car was at least a hundred feet from the Lighthouse.

Which made absolutely no sense, because I knew that I'd parked directly beside it when I'd driven up. I remembered that. I fucking remembered that!

I ran back to the door and slammed my fists against it, hitting it again and again as tears burst from my eyes. Why was this happening!

With no movement at all from the door, I went back to the window and looked, rubbing my eyes in confusion over what had occurred outside.

The car was another fifty feet further away. It looked as though it had been abandoned for years, the body having rusted away, and roots, grass, and shrubs were growing all over and all throughout. The longer I looked, the more I realized something was happening at the car.

The roots.

They were actively squirming, growing, and wrapping around the car as I watched.

Even though I knew the car was completely useless and a pile of rusted junk, something inside me screamed that I needed to save it, that if I wanted any chance of surviving this strange place, the car needed to be freed from the roots that were destroying it further. I raced to the door, grabbed it, and yanked and yanked and yanked. *Fucking open!* It wasn't moving, so I kicked it and elbowed it and hit my hip against it and instead of the door magically opening, my entire body burned with agony and the pain told me to stop being a fool and to stop hitting the door.

When I had parked beside the Lighthouse, I had stopped almost directly beside the door, right outside. Now when I looked at the car, I saw it was close to two hundred feet away.

A sense of dread overtook my body. I thought about that calendar. *Was it a key to this madness?* I raced up the stairs as fast as I could. Once at the landing, I ran to the calendar, ignoring the subtle tingle that I had started to feel in my leg again.

I needed to see.

The calendar was still on the wall.
The image was still the Lighthouse.
The month was still July.
But the year had changed to 1984.

11.

There was a time in my life where I felt like I alienated everyone around me. Where nobody understood who *I* was or why *I* was. That the me wasn't the me for them. So, I turned my attention to the two things I could tangibly mold, and that accepted me for who I was: music and sports.

I sought out artists who were unconventional and not exactly "pop". Some of them had singles that became chart toppers and some of them were bone fide superstars, but they still wrote music that spoke to me in a way others didn't. In my youth, my dad had played a lot of the older, classic artists. And through this, I had gained a love of newer artists who sounded old. In my teens, I discovered some of the most amazing music, and every new CD that I put in the CD player, introduced me to new and exciting worlds, both musically and artistically. The booklets that came with them would constantly knock my socks off. I'd spend hours examining artwork and reading the lyrics. Those two components acted as a bridge between what I heard and what I felt inside. I knew I wasn't alone in this practice, that generations had done the exact same thing throughout every decade, but in those moments, alone in my room, it was all new to me.

All my constant feelings of being alone had completely closed me off from a lot of the 'potential out there.

Which made my decision the hardest decision I've ever made.

Seeing the weight of my words crush the love of my life hurt my soul, but in a weird way it affirmed to me that I was doing the right thing.

I can still remember the day I first saw *Her*.

She was leaving the school we both attended, through a side door, at the end of our one long hallway. I was on the far side of the parking lot, sitting on a cement block that doubled as a barrier between the lot and the road on the other side, deep in conversation with a friend when she walked out.

And I had a movie moment.

I know it sounds corny, but at that moment, as she stepped outside, the sun hit her flowing blonde hair, the wind blew her dress around her and then she looked directly at me, her green eyes piercing my heart from fifty feet away.

A few days later we were going steady, as the kids used to say, and somehow through the isolation I'd weighed myself down with, I'd found a light in the dark.

We shared everything with each other, telling each other our lives up until that moment, and we discovered that we had a mutual love of music.

We remained together throughout the rest of high school, and when I graduated and moved for college, we made things work. While it wasn't technically a long-distance relationship, I was a two-hour drive away, so we spoke on the phone each night and I'd drive back every weekend, where we'd spend as much time together as we could.

We moved in together when I was entering my third year of college, and never looked back. Through thick and thin, we've been a constant in each other's lives, making the other one smile every day.

When we moved once more so that I could finish my degree, we started attending concerts weekly, our love of music a shared passion. We spent our time watching TV shows we loved and going to the gym, and we even adopted an amazing American Bulldog who brightened our lives and gave us memories that will last a lifetime.

During our first discussion, where I laid out the facts and went over what I thought was best and how I thought she should handle it, she wouldn't hear it. I pleaded my case, saying we needed to act now, before it was too late, but she steadfastly refused. I was frustrated, but I understood. So, I remained patient, until I couldn't take it anymore.

And that was when I packed the car and drove.

And that was where you all came in.

12.

It had been snowing non-stop since I'd raced from that parking lot on the top of the mountain. The drive since had been a mix of a white-knuckle roller-coaster and a sobbing, anxiety-filled panic attack. The road had been nothing but winding as I descended the mountain, the degree steep enough that signs warned for large trucks to shift down, and a half-dozen times I'd seen long runaway lanes climbing high up the hillside as I zipped by.

My mind kept trying to remind me that something had rushed from within the woods, that there had been a massive beast trying to rip me apart, but I pushed those thoughts away, trying to remain focused on the road.

That determination wasn't enough, though, as I had to actively pump the brake pedal repeatedly, each corner coming fast and seemingly sharper than the last. When a strange shadow caught my attention along the side of the car, I immediately believed the creature had somehow chased me down, and without thinking things through logically – exhaustion and lethargy will do that – I slammed my foot on the gas pedal, the car rocketing forward at a dangerous clip.

The next corner approached fast, and I pulled my foot from the gas pedal, then tapped the brake, feeling the car shift and slide, the road conditions continuing to disintegrate. With each tap of the brake, the entire car shuddered, the back-end fishtailing just enough to spike my adrenaline and fill my mind with the very real possibility that I'd be crashing into the side of the mountain.

I'd grown up where we received heavy snow every winter. My mom was afraid of driving in the snow, but my dad had no qualms, and taught me early to steer into the skid. He'd frequently give me driving tips, even before I received my license, and a few times he'd even had me purposefully drive into situations to drive out of them. Those lessons always took place up a dirt road away from the highway.

With that in mind, I knew I only had one real chance to not slam into the rocky hills that hugged the side of the road. I'd need to slam the brakes hard and drive through the expected skid. The car would slide, maybe even spin, but if I kept my wits about me, I'd be able to maneuver the vehicle and come out unscathed. I had just enough time to hype myself up before I slammed the brake pedal.

The result was immediate.

The brakes locked and the car went into a violent, twisting spin.

I tried my best to find something my eyes could stay on, much like a figure skater during their spins, wanting to prevent disorientation. The car was traveling too fast and spinning too fast for me to do that, so I focused on trying to steer the car out of the spin and down the road. The ditch wouldn't be an ideal place to die. Especially after having just survived an almost-attack from whatever that thing was.

I needed to get the car under control, and soon. I pumped the brakes, holding the wheel tighter before steering with the spin and giving the gas pedal a gentle press. I thought I was gaining the upper hand, but then the car spun even more, as though what I'd tried specifically to do made it worse, and I knew then that this was it, this was the end. I braced for impact, the ditch the last thing I saw in front of me before I closed my eyes.

But no impact came.

Instead, the car spun once more, slowed, and came to a stop facing back up the mountain.

I hadn't looked in the mirror once since leaving the pullout, and now that I was facing that direction, I knew I couldn't look. *It would be there.* Standing there, breathing heavily from chasing me. Waiting to unleash its viciousness only after eye contact was made.

The corner ahead – well, technically behind me – had a perception of safety. As though, if I could drive the car around that corner, the beast wouldn't be able to get to me. It might've been nothing but false hope, but it was all I had, and the main reason I needed to turn the car around and get out of there.

With the fear that the icy road would prevent me from a timely escape, I put the car in reverse and gently gave it some gas. The car responded, inching forward. Taking that as a sign to get going, I steered the car around one-eighty, and I did it all without looking at what loomed a few hundred feet up the road. Driving away at a reasonable speed, I couldn't help but smile when I rounded the first corner and was met with a straight downhill section. It'd put more distance between myself and the thing that chased me. Before I fully turned the corner, I steeled myself and glanced in the mirror, finding nothing standing where I was certain something would've been.

The reality that nothing was there surprised me. *Was I losing my mind? Had I gone crazy, and I didn't know it?*

I made the decision then, for my sanity at least, that the only way to really ensure I would remain in control, was a two-pronged approach. First, I lowered both front windows. Then I cranked the music, singing along immediately. This felt safe, familiar, and I'd be able to at least remain focused on the road and what I could physically see in front of the car.

Even with the window down and the music blaring, a yawn snuck up on me. Looking at the clock on the dash, I saw it'd been almost an hour since I left the pullout, but it felt as though I'd been driving for far longer. I was concerned that my gas gauge hadn't moved. There was no way that the car *was* that efficient on fuel.

Pushing that worry away, I turned my attention to the fact that the snow had stopped for the moment, and with the windows down, the cool breeze was refreshing. I shifted in my seat, my bladder letting me know that I'd need to stop soon, and that was followed very soon after by my belly grumbling. Even after those two bodily signals, I knew full well why I wasn't stopping. Each of the last two times I'd stopped, I'd almost been ripped limb from limb.

If I was going to stop, and the truth was I'd need to soon, I needed a plan.

I was too afraid to leave the vehicle. As I ran some scenarios through my mind, a road sign caught my attention ahead on the right.

Slowing so that I could read it, I felt a rush of hope as the words were processed. *Fuel 5*. Below, *Edgewater 205*. I couldn't help but smile, just a bit. It was as though I'd won the lottery, and best of all, there'd be a bathroom. Or at least, I hoped there would be. *What if it's not open?* The only reason that thought even crossed my mind was because I was up high on the mountain, in the middle of nowhere, and having not seen a car in what felt like weeks, there was a very real chance that the business was closed permanently. I rolled the windows halfway up and pushed the nagging pressure of my bladder out of my head.

As the car rounded what I hoped would be the last corner before I arrived at the gas station, dark clouds loomed in the distance. *That's not good*. Even from where I was, I could see the storm brewing, and the clouds moving rapidly in my direction. As if on cue, snow began to fall once again, the flakes thick and dense. I flipped the wipers on and closed the windows completely, but before my mood completely soured, my eyes caught sight of the building ahead.

There it was.

The gas station.

And to my relief, the lights were on, a truck parked near the lone set of pumps out front. I slowed and pulled into the gas station lot.

I fished for my wallet, a sudden urge to vomit hitting me when I wondered if I'd left it in my piss-soaked jeans back at the rest stop. When my fingers closed around the old, grainy leather, I let out a sigh of relief. I tried to prepare myself for how my legs would feel when I got out of the car, but instead it was the cold blast of air that almost knocked me over. I went around to the other side of the car, flipped open the gas flap, but only when I squeezed the nozzle did I realize the pump wasn't working. Re-racking the nozzle, I walked to the door, half expecting to find it locked, but when I pushed the door inwards, it swung open easily, and the chime of a bell above the door sounded. Inside, I was thankful for the warm air that circulated, but even so, I still rubbed my hands together. I hadn't been outside long, but it had been enough time for my hands to grow cold. The opening strains of a song – the kind you'd only hear playing in a gas station – began in the background on whatever radio station was considered local. I looked around the interior, taking in what the place had to offer, but didn't see anyone stocking the shelves, or behind the counter.

"Hello?"

I could've screamed.

I'd not heard the young woman come up beside me. It'd been days since I'd spoken to anyone, or had anyone talk to me, so when her voice broke the silence, it was too much. I shuddered and just barely prevented myself from screaming. But then a different emotion flowed through me. Elation. A person stood there, a real person, and they had spoken to me and they were still there, and they didn't look like they were a gargantuan beast ready to rip me apart. I felt my eyes well up.

"Oh wow, am I ever glad to see you! So much has happened, I didn't think I was even going to make it here. I thought for sure I was gonna run out of gas! And I can't remember the last time I ate, and there was this beast, this thing that chased me in the woods, and I spun around in the car and –"

She didn't even glance at me.

I just babbled on and on, needing to get everything out, to verbally expel everything that had happened, which to tell the truth, was way more than I'd thought. And even then, I still wasn't sure over how long this had taken place. I just needed to speak and get this anxious weight off my chest. After I finished, and breathed out a comically long breath, she went behind the counter and looked outside through the dirt-caked window. From where I stood, I was able to watch as her facial expressions shifted and changed. Her eyes went wide as she saw something out there, but when she turned to look at me, I felt my heartbeat stop and a cold shiver race down my spine.

How was this even possible?

It was *Her*.

Her.

The love of my life.

I never thought I'd see her gorgeous green eyes again.

I never thought I would see that cute little nose or those perfectly formed lips. I knew my decision would haunt me forever, and that by abandoning and leaving, I would pay a very steep price, which made me wonder if this was some strange, twisted joke? A cruel form of punishment?

I blinked and she was gone. Someone else stood in *Her* place.

She wasn't *Her*. Her hair *was* similar, and her face *was* similar. She may have even been one of her relatives, but it wasn't *Her*. My heart dropped when it became clear.

The lady was staring at me. More accurately, this lady was staring *through* me. Almost like I wasn't there at all.

Almost like I was transparent.

13.

"Hello?"

My tongue was so heavy, that when I spoke, the word came out closer to a croak. I felt like a ghost in a movie, trying to let someone know I was there, but getting no response.

I was going to wave my hand, try to get her attention again, when she blinked and cocked her head to the left.

"Sorry, my mind was preoccupied for a moment."

I let out a breath I'd anxiously held, wondering for the shortest of moments if this woman was real. But even after hearing her speak, I knew something was off. I just wasn't sure what.

"Yes, sorry to startle you. You were in the back when I came in, I guess."

The interior of the gas station was unremarkable.

In the middle was shelving carrying a variety of chips and chocolate bars, a rack nearby, stocked with horribly overpriced toiletries and necessities. The kind that you inevitably forget to pack and have to spend twice the normal cost to replace. On the wall nearest the door, a freezer was situated against the wall. When I was a kid, that was always the first place I'd go at the local corner store. Just down from there, a magazine rack was against the wall. Beside that, an ATM, that would gouge each user with insane convenience fees and beside the ATM, the door to the washroom that looked as though it'd never been wiped down once. Even from where I stood, I could see old trials of water where wet hands had closed it behind them.

The other walls were home to the beverage coolers, and contained an assortment of cola's, energy drinks, and dairy products, and in the last two, a mix of beer and wine. Back at the front of the store, directly beside the front counter was a deli that advertised sandwiches *MADE FRESH DAILY!* Even with the exclamation mark for posterity, I knew, and everyone else who entered knew, there was no chance in hell that was possible.

Looking back at the lady, I was met with the same expression, same tilted angle of her head, and I noticed her eyes seemed overly white. *Was she blind?*

"I'm not blind, asshole."

It was uncanny. Almost like she'd read my mind.

"I didn't read your mind."

I started to say something, just wanting something to come out of my mouth and cut through the awkward moment, but she broke the silence instead.

"Well, technically I'm legally blind, but I can see some shapes and objects. Just very limited details. And I can see you looking at me."

"Wow," I replied "That's impressive. You're so functional. There's so much in here. You keep it so clean and organized."

"Thanks. My dad owns the place, has since it opened twenty years ago. I've pretty much grown up here, walking these aisles and memorizing each product by its length, weight, and packaging."

I let out a long, impressed whistle, which caused us both to laugh.

"So, stranger, what can I help you with?"

I really only needed gas and a few snacks to tide me over.

The events of the last few days had essentially zapped my appetite, but I knew I needed to get something in me, and it may as well be sugar loaded. At the same time, it'd been almost three days since I had spoken to anyone, let alone had a normal conversation, and I was enjoying this. The alternative was driving alone in my car.

"I definitely need to fill up. Not sure how the car made it all this way actually. And I'll grab some snacks for the ride. But to be perfectly honest with you, I haven't talked with anyone for the last few days, so, if it's all the same to you, I'll get one of those fresh sandwiches and maybe sit and chat for a bit?"

As the last word hung in the air, I could've died. I felt like such a moron asking if we could chat, but at that point, I just didn't want to be sitting in the car alone again. It was like I was asking her out on a date, and I expected her to deny my request. Thankfully when I turned my head to see her reaction, she had a small but distinguishable smile on her face.

"You know what," she replied, "I haven't had anyone stop by in, well, as long as I can remember. If you don't mind if I eat as well, that sounds like a great plan!"

I smiled back and went to the deli. After looking over everything, I selected a turkey and cheese sandwich on whole wheat bread with mayo. Judging from the ingredients, this looked like the best choice for something that tasted delicious. *It'd be better than hospital food*, I told myself, while I grabbed a root beer and a big jug of water from the nearest cooler. As I walked back over, I also grabbed a bag of chips, a couple chocolate bars, and a bag of Twizzlers for good measure, setting them on the counter.

"May as well pay."

Like a magician, I watched as she correctly identified each item and the cost. She even told me it was a better deal to get two bags of Twizzlers, which was a deal I wasn't about to pass up.

Retrieving my wallet, I handed her the cash, and while she grabbed my change from the register, I stuffed everything but the root beer and the sandwich into a shopping bag.

"I'll throw this in the car first and come back and eat. And please, don't let me forget to grab gas before I leave," I said, as I turned towards the door.

"STOP!"

She yelled so loudly and suddenly, that I almost dropped the bag. I turned to see why she was hollering at me.

"You can't go outside right now," she said. "Something's out there. Something's waiting for you."

14.

I froze as I was instantly transported back to that pullout.

How was this even possible?

I knew exactly what was waiting for me outside. That *thing*. But how could it still be coming for me? I'd driven what I perceived to be a far distance since leaving. And yet, according to this lady, it had caught up and was waiting for me outside.

I thought back to how afraid I'd been at that sign in the ditch.

How scared I was at the pullout.

But hearing her tell me it was waiting outside, catapulted me back almost forty years to a time I'd long forgotten. Now, in this moment it came rushing back.

It brought me back to the time I saw my first wolverine.

Growing up, my grandfather had a trap-line. He had it for years before I came along, and I believe his father had it before him. It was a section of land, a trail really, through about ten kilometers of wilderness. It was accessible only by snowshoe for many years, and later you could drive alongside some of it, accessing the far end by snowmobile.

When I was a young boy, every Saturday morning during the winter months, I'd be dropped off at my grandparents down the street from us. My grandpa and dad would load up the snowmobile and then we'd head off to check and reset the traps. It was common to catch everything from lynx, squirrels, fox, and even the occasional mink. My grandpa would skin the animals and sell them to fur traders. By doing this, he was able to collect a little pocket change. Growing up in an isolated area, we were bridging the old world with the new world. Using what the land provided for us, as well as having some early modern technology.

A few times, myself, or one of my sisters and I, would go with them. We would stay in the truck while they took the sleds. I stopped going with them when I became too afraid of the narrowness of the road. I would have a panic attack when we had to do a ten point turn on a road just wide enough for one vehicle, with a straight drop down a steep hill on one side.

After a few years of not going, I came to a crossroads. I was five or six at the time, and realized that tough guys need to get over their fears. Why I thought that I have no idea, but it was something that resonated in my young brain and became something I needed to overcome. So, the next weekend, I asked if I could go. "Sure," my grandpa enthusiastically replied, not knowing what he already had in store for me. We loaded up the sleds in the back of the truck, and off we went. I felt strong, brave, and macho, and I was ready to take on the world.

We arrived at the first trap, which was about fifty feet off the side of the road, just up a short rocky bank. My grandpa turned and asked if I wanted to run up there and check it myself. Did I ever! I hopped from the truck, ran up the side of the hill and came around the tree, finding the trap.

Nothing.

It was empty.

The trap was still set and baited, so I left it, ran back down, and climbed in the truck.

"Nothing," I almost shouted at him, amazed at how grown up I'd become. *I'll probably start shaving soon*, I thought. We stopped at the next fifteen or so traps and found them all empty.

"Getting near the end of the season," my grandpa said. "Let's check the next one and if it's empty, we'll call it a day and head back."

I was devastated.

My chance to show my grandpa I wasn't scared of anything anymore was about to disappear. It was one thing for me to join him, but it was a completely different thing for me to retrieve an animal from the traps and help him skin it.

One left.

My last hope.

All I wanted was for a small squirrel or even a weasel to be in there. I'd pop it out of the trap and if it was still alive, I'd bop it on its head, like I'd seen my grandpa do before. Then I would walk back with my trophy, a hero in the world's eyes. Little did I know, the outcome of the last trap would be very different than what my small brain imagined.

We parked the truck at the end of the road. This was the last trap we could walk to, and my grandpa figured if there was nothing here, there was no reason to unload the snowmobile to check the others. He was planning on picking up the remainder the following weekend, and would just leave them baited until then.

I jumped from the truck, with more pep, in my now, man-like steps, and walked to the hill with my grandpa. My excitement put me a few steps ahead, so I approached the trap on the other side of the tree first. All I saw was a blur of motion, with a loud snarl and snapping of teeth, as something came flying out from the trap directly at me.

I froze.

All traces of machismo had evaporated in an instant, as I reverted to a very small, very scared boy. The *blur* thankfully had its back leg and tail stuck in the trap, and as it came screaming through the air towards me, it came to a halt just inches from my face before it was jolted back. By this time, my grandpa had made it around the tree and grabbed me, pulling me back from the animal. I couldn't take my eyes from the creature. It was the scariest thing I'd ever seen. Years later I'd see those eyes again when I first watched 'The Neverending Story' and Gmork was introduced. What felt like an eternity passed, as it tried to wiggle free before turning and lunging at me once more. I knew at that moment, even as young as I was, that this was no cartoon. If I freed it, to ease its pain, it would rip my throat open. It wouldn't lick my face in thanks and race away into the trees. No, it had only one thing blazing in its eyes, and that was 'kill the little one.' When my grandpa said that I could go back to the truck, I didn't need any coaxing. I probably ran, though that part is fuzzy. I do remember getting into the truck, climbing into the back seat, and pulling the old blanket he kept in the back of that blue Ford truck over my head. I was crying immediately.

My grandpa, meanwhile, had grabbed his rifle from the gun rack on the back window. The anticipation of the crack of the gun hung in the air, and when it came, it seemed so loud, as though it was going to start an avalanche of snow or a stampede of animals. A few moments later, there was a loud THUNK from the back of the truck, the door opened, and the gun was re-racked. I was still under the blanket. The moments ticked by, until finally my grandpa cleared his throat and said, "I'm sorry I sent you up there before me."

We didn't say another word on the drive back.

I remained under the blanket, feeling ashamed.

I didn't think I could ever show my face in front of my family again. A family of loggers, hunters, fishermen, and trappers. I'd be disowned and never spoken to again.

Once back at my grandpa's, he parked the truck and asked if I wanted to see the animal now that it couldn't hurt me. I didn't answer, so he said he'd get my mom and when I was ready, he'd show me. But only when I was ready.

Not long after, my mom came to the truck and told me that everything was ok, that she was there, and that there was nothing to be ashamed of.

I slowly crawled out, but stopped when I saw my grandpa. He walked over, ruffled my hair, and said, "Look at it this way, you came face-to-face with a wolverine and won."

I had no idea what that meant, but I told him I was ready to see the animal. Even knowing that it was dead, when he showed me it, I thought it was the scariest thing I'd ever seen. It had a small fox-like snout with pointed teeth and long sharp claws on each foot. Years later, I learned more about the wolverine and thought, *if I'd have known this back then, I probably would've had a heart attack*. The animal is a vicious creature, with nothing but muscle covering its tiny forty-pound body.

The fear I'd felt then was the worst I'd ever felt.

Until now.

When the woman had told me to not go outside because something was waiting for me, my blood ran cold.

"What do you mean?"

She paused, studying my face. I knew she was formulating a response, one that wouldn't cause me to freak out.

There was a mutual understanding between us, that things would never be the same once she replied.

"There's a black... *mass* that's seeking you. It's been coming every night for as long as I can remember, and even though it never enters, it still comes right up to the window. I knew it was looking for you even before I ever knew who you were. I'd been expecting you for some time."

I stared at her.

Every response that came to me wasn't a response I wanted to put out into the world. So, instead, I clenched my jaw, keeping my mouth shut. As I worked through what to say, a neon green cooler at the back of the store caught my attention.

I thought a light was malfunctioning inside, as it flickered and darkened, flickered and darkened, but after the darkness seemed to fill up more of the reflection with each subsequent flash, I realized it was reflecting the black mass outside as it approached the window. It was directly outside, looking in, looking for me.

"Quick, over here!" she yelled.

I ran to her, diving behind the counter, abandoning my sandwich and drink.

In my haste to hide, I dove to the far corner, completely blocking my view of the window. I couldn't see anything, which wasn't good. I needed to see out, needed to see if the mass was still there, looming like a hurricane on the horizon.

As the mass pushed against the glass, the windowpane elicited a sharp cracking sound. The woman had started to pretend as though it was just her there, going about how she'd normally act if it was just her. She wiped down the countertop, and moved my sandwich and root beer off to the side, before cleaning where they'd been. She grabbed a bucket, filled it in the small sink behind the deli cooler, and, using a squeegee, started to clean the glass doors of the coolers, beginning with the farthest one. I stayed huddled in the corner, knowing that she was cleaning as far from where I hid as possible, drawing whatever it was outside to look towards her. *My car is parked outside.* That was the only thing that still suggested somebody else was there, but I couldn't see what the thing outside was doing, so I had no idea if it'd lost interest in looking within, or if it was still actively searching.

As if in reply to my thoughts, the windows above the counter groaned and flexed as something massive leaned against them.

My mind raced. All I could picture was a massive, hairy beast, leaving against the glass, hoping to find me and catch me. I tried to move even further against the wall, but couldn't. The first inklings of a panic attack started to well up deep in my body, my sweat glands working in overdrive. With the distinct sensation of the world closing in around me, I was finding it difficult to stay against the wall, the building seemingly pushing me away from it, out in front of the seeking eyes of the black mass.

This is it, I thought.

Trapped, with nowhere to turn, nowhere to run, I accepted the fact that the last thing I'd ever see would be the fluorescent lights within the gas station.

Then I heard the lady humming a familiar tune, but one I couldn't place.

It had a slow melody, its rhythm filling my heart with warmth.

My body relaxed.

Somehow, she'd picked up on my impending panic attack and was helping to bring me down off that ledge. If I went over, I'd never come back.

She kept humming, and as she did so, she subtly found my reflection in the cooler, making eye contact with me. When she saw I was looking back, she smiled.

She continued working her way from cooler to cooler, humming as she went, cleaning each one with efficient movements.

I had no idea if the beast was still at the glass, and I didn't care.

Her humming had me hypnotized, and oddly, I realized I was growing drowsy. She'd progressed to the windows at the front of the store, and as she cleaned, I tried to keep my eyes open. Every time I looked towards her, she shimmered, as though she was only coming through in waves. I felt my head nod and bob, losing the fight to stay awake. I was comfortable. I was content. Safe. I looked and found her cleaning the glass of the front doors. Then she was opening the front doors.

My brain screamed at me. Didn't I see? Couldn't I understand?

She was opening them to let the black mass in.

She'd drugged me and now the beast would come in and it was game over.

I heard footsteps approaching. My eyes remained heavier than they'd ever been before, but I could hear the footsteps come around the counter. I couldn't open my eyes, and when I tried to speak, all I forced out through numb lips was, 'Uuuh-hhhhhh.'

The steps seemed too soft for the beast, and when it took my head in its hands, I was surprised how delicate they were.

Using the last ounce of strength I had, I opened my eyes just enough to see that it wasn't the beast in front of me, but the woman.

"You can sleep," she said. "It's moved on."

I felt her lean in and gently kiss my cheek as sleep fully embraced me.

15.

Nothing made sense.

How was the car so far from the Lighthouse?

What was happening with the calendar?

And why was I standing here, with my right side numb?

Was someone outside? Had they moved the car? Were they the source of that fucking godawful noise that was plaguing me?

Maybe they'd barricaded the front door?

That would make sense, wouldn't it? Wouldn't it? Wouldn't it? Wouldn't it?

Jesus, I had to get a hold of myself, I was losing it. I'm losing it right? Right?

Fuck. Ok, I need to just go back up a level or two and look out, see if I could see some asshole darting around, pretending he was in some sort of real-life video game and actively making my life hell. But I couldn't go. Couldn't move. My body was rock solid. Stuck where it was, standing, staring at the calendar, unwilling to respond to my desire to move.

But now that I couldn't move, another thought ran through my mind. Maybe another person was here, inside the Lighthouse, and they'd somehow drugged me and preventing me from moving. And they'd snuck over here and changed the calendar.

It can't be, I thought. Nobody else is here. It's just me.

Me and this calendar. This calendar that I could see changing before my eyes.

Watching, the image at first looked like water had been spilt on it, the ink running, but instead of blurring and distorting, a new image emerged. It was me, on the deck at the top of the Lighthouse, an immense shadow blotting out the sun.

I had to move. I grabbed the chair to my left and pulled, wanting to use it as a lever and force my body away from where I stood. Slowly, my body responded, which I was thrilled with, as the other alternative would've seen me falling to the floor. My right foot moved forward, then my left, then as my muscle control returned, I was able to shuffle across the room, back to the stairs.

Every step I took on my return to the top level was exhausting and frustrating. My body was tired, my mind even more so, a level of disbelief hanging heavy over my thoughts. I expected to fall. Over and over again. Every time I shifted my weight from one leg to the next, I tensed, preparing for my leg to give out and for me to topple backwards. I wasn't sure if I'd find any answers up there, but at least I could take a look outside and try to figure out what in the fuck was happening.

Or I wouldn't.

That was the train of thought I was starting to lean towards as I moved closer to the top landing. Like everything else in this godforsaken Lighthouse, I'd be met with more questions than answers.

Once at the top landing, I scooted across the bed and pushed the doors open. As I went to step out onto the deck, my right side tingled, a reminder that the numbness and weakness could return without warning. I shook my leg, making sure my foot felt fine, before I walked to the railing and looked around the curvature of the Lighthouse as far as I comfortably could.

From where I stood, my car was able to be seen, but only because it had moved even further back from when I last saw it.

More changes had taken place.

The car was completely engulfed by the foliage.

I leaned as far over the edge of the railing as I could, looking in desperation for any sign that somebody was out there, somebody responsible for the insanity that was occurring. Of course, that would only explain the car, and wouldn't reveal any of the secrets about what was happening within the Lighthouse itself, but I didn't care. One solid answer was better than nothing, and if I got the answer about the car, I could return my focus to the source of the noise, and what was taking place several landings below me. While looking, I felt the first rain drops on my arm. Looking up at the sky, I was shocked to see a swarm of deep black clouds that covered the sky. No light was visible through the clouds. So dark were they that it gave the impression that the day had become night. The rain increased in volume as I stood there, and as I went to the other side of the deck, it was falling so hard that the drops felt closer to small pellets of hail.

There was still no sign of anybody around the car, and the longer I looked, the more convinced I was that there wasn't anybody out there at all. As the rain fell harder, I decided to suspend my futile search and go back inside, not wanting to get soaked.

Heading back in, I stopped halfway, looking at the large glass dome that encased the top of the Lighthouse. I knew that within that dome, I'd have an unimpeded 360-degree view around the outside of the Lighthouse. If there *was* someone out there, that would be the perfect place to look from. *No time like the present*, I thought. As though a switch had been thrown, I felt reinvigorated. I practically sprinted inside, jumping onto the bed. My wet shoes left two big splotches on the blanket, but I didn't care. I needed to get up there now. I bounded to the spiral staircase, ignoring the tingle that barely registered in my leg. I didn't have time for my body not to work, so I mentally pushed past that, doing what needed to be done and not giving my body an opportunity to not cooperate. At the stairs, I looked up, wondering if a dark shadow would be looking down, but when all I saw was an empty staircase, I started up, wondering if I'd kill two birds with one stone. Would I discover the source of the noise AND find who was messing with my car at the same time? I could only hope.

At the apex of the stairs, I came to a door made of opaque glass. Whether it was real or not, I wasn't sure, but judging by the age of the Lighthouse, I assumed it was. It had the look of being *original*, which caused me to gently turn the handle, not wanting to break it. The door swung open easily, and, stepping through, I entered the circular glass room. I gasped in awe when my eyes fell upon the huge round light that filled up the middle of the space. It was perhaps the most impressive light I'd ever seen, and I could only imagine what it looked like at night when it was lit up.

On the opposite side was a desk with a stool, and beyond that nothing but water as far as the eye could see. Approaching the desk, I found it littered with nautical maps and schedules. A pair of binoculars sat on the window ledge, easily within reach from the stool. And that was it. Nothing else was in the room, nothing that could've been the source of that noise.

My heart dropped.

It was as though an anchor had been tied to the hopes of finding those answers, and when none came, the anchor had been thrown overboard.

This *had* to be where the noise was coming from. I wanted to scream. I wanted to hurl the huge light through the window and watch it smash into a million pieces upon the rocky shore below. But I didn't. Instead, I went to the desk and haphazardly flipped through the various maps and papers, looking for something, *anything*, that might give me some direction. I was grasping at straws, desperate for an explanation.

Seeing the binoculars sitting there, I grabbed them and went to the other side of the space, finding my car far out in the field. Wiping the dust from the lenses, I raised them to my eyes, took a second to focus, and when the image came into detail, I let out a frustrated breath.

It was even further away, and covered in moss and roots that intertwined throughout the body. I could see the seats had decomposed, exposing the rusted springs and frame below.

I looked around the area near the car, spotting movement that excited me for a second, until I realized it was two seagulls fighting over a scrap. On the other side of the two birds were close to another dozen seagulls, all gathered around, like they were watching some sort of seagull gladiator event, placing bets on who would win.

Returning my attention to my car, I struggled to find it. I lowered the binoculars and rubbed my eyes and looked towards where it had been. I saw it still sitting there, which made me wonder why I wasn't finding it with the binoculars. But as I searched, I thought I saw something move not far from the car, an odd shifting that my eyes registered but my brain didn't recognize. Raising the binoculars, I looked.

What was that?

I moved around, adjusting the zoom on the binoculars, focusing and refocusing on area after area around the car. I was doing a grid sweep, trying to not miss anything, when the binoculars' gaze fell upon some shrubs. That set alarm bells ringing in my head. First, I'd not previously seen any shrubs around that spot. Second, they looked like shrubs, but not *real* shrubs. Something about them was unnatural.

The longer I looked, the more I started to see through the shrubs. Not past them, but *through* them, my eyes finding the space between the branches and the leaves. The longer I looked, the more I understood it was being filled by something big. Something immense, that lumbered and swayed back and forth.

I froze.

It was as though I'd become glued to the spot, unable to lower the binoculars and look away.

This massive... *thing* was holding up shrubbery to meekly hide behind as it shuffled towards the Lighthouse. As though it could feel that I'd spotted it in the distance, it lowered the shrubs.

"What?" I said aloud, my voice cracking. Whether due to fright or that I hadn't said anything in hours, I wasn't sure, but as I watched, the dark shape grew taller and taller, towering over the shrubs.

At the crest of the horizon, close enough that finer nightmarish details were becoming visible, there was a monstrous *CRACK!* The sound was so massive that it shook me where I stood, a queasiness overcoming me for a split second. A second CRACK sounded, this one seemingly coming from lower in the Lighthouse, which made me wonder what in the hell was going on. Even as my mind raced, another *BANG* came, a sound so loud and so fierce from the belly of the Lighthouse that I could only imagine someone, or *something* had just rammed through the front door.

This seemed to loosen me enough that I was able to set the binoculars down, pushing away the reality that my left arm was losing its strength and sensation. A feeling of dread washed over me. Someone else was actually inside the Lighthouse with me, and if they weren't going to attack me, that fucking black monster outside was surely going to.

I was petrified. I'd have thought there would've been some level of excitement, to once and for all find an answer, but instead it was pure terror. *If I don't fall down the stairs and break my neck, whatever awaits me at the bottom is going to devour me,* I thought as I hustled down.

THUMP!

A louder and more violent sound erupted, and for a moment I wondered if it was a warning, the source trying to tell me to stay away and not go down any further.

As the sound echoed around in my ears, my right leg gave out and I stumbled down the last few steps, crashing to the floor at the kitchen level. At the same time, three levels above me, the deafening noise repeated, but instead of one single sound it was three quick reports, each louder than the last. The final one was so extreme, I could feel my bones vibrate against each other.

THUMP, THUMP, ***THUMP!***

What in the hell was happening?

16.

Blinking, I looked up at the roof, which was an odd thing to be looking at.

An ache bloomed in the back of my head as I tried to remember what had happened.

I knew something was wrong when I tried to sit, and pain erupted all over. That was followed by a cold numbness slithering across my arms and down my torso, finally engulfing my legs.

My brain was telling my body to move, but nothing was happening.

This wasn't good, and as I lay there, I felt a rising panic. But what could I do about it?

I was stranded on my back, staring straight up at the ceiling. This was the closest I'd ever had to an out-of-body experience. In my mind I could picture what I looked like from above, and if I hadn't been on the verge of completely freaking out, I would've laughed at the absurdity of my situation.

Somewhere nearby, a noise caught my attention. At first it was a dull thing, devoid of emotion. But when it happened a second time, and a third and a fourth, that changed. As the cadence came faster, and the viciousness increased, I understood that it was the sound of something desperately trying to bring this structure down on itself.

On me.

I was going to die.

Every ounce of me believed that.

And with that horrendous realization came something else.

Adrenaline.

Deep within my physiological system, neurons and synapses activated, sending signals down the motor pathways. Muscle cells fired, and to my surprise, my body responded. At first it was just a tingling sensation in both feet. Then it travelled up my legs, across my torso and over my arms. Finally, I regained the ability to turn my head, and I was able to look down the staircase beside me at the main entrance below.

It was when my eyes fell upon the cracked wood that had exploded inwards, from whatever had smashed through it, that everything came back.

Whatever had destroyed the door had to have been large, which made me think it was the same dark mass that I'd seen approaching. It had covered the distance from the car to the Lighthouse quickly, but that didn't surprise me, based on how big it had been. But, truthfully, in this strange building, I was slowly starting to comprehend the idea that not everything was how it seemed. That time and space had no rhyme or rhythm. That what was happening from moment to moment, might be happening at a different speed elsewhere.

My mind went back to that calendar. Did it play a bigger role in this chaos than I'd originally thought?

Tingling all over my body let me know that feeling was returning. It reminded me of those times I'd played far too long in the snow and then would hop straight into a scalding hot bath. I was able to roll onto one side, but stopped as soon as I felt a line of drool leak from my mouth. It was as though I'd just left the dentist's chair, my mouth still numb from the freezing.

Rotating around so that I ended up on my knees, I tentatively stood. I expected somewhere on my body to flare up from pain, but surprisingly it was just my back that reacted, letting me know it was stiff and sore. That suggested I'd been on the floor longer than I'd previously thought.

Something shifted high above me. It hadn't made the same commotion as the thumping, but the noise was loud enough to get my attention and force the question upon me.

What now?

I felt like this had been the struggle I'd been stuck in since arriving at this place. Do I go up and try and find out what made the noise, or do I somehow get outside and figure out what was happening to the car?

I didn't think there was an honest-to-God better option, a 'this way shall bring you answers' route.

So, I followed my curiosity.

I decided that once and for all, I had to find out what the source of that noise was.

It was time to get to the bottom of this insanity and move on. Hell, I hadn't even begun to go through the checklist of things that needed to be done. Though, I'd not seen it anywhere, which didn't seem correct.

Going to the stairs, I wanted to punch myself all over, to hit my legs and my arms and my body and tell it to do its fucking job, to not fail me and to be there when I needed it most. But I knew I couldn't trust it, knew that no matter how much I hammered on my thighs, if the muscles decided to not support me, there really was nothing I could do about it.

Taking each step with slow, purposeful foot positioning, I held onto the railing and began to ascend. As I passed the window facing the direction of my once operable car, I caught movement from the corner of my eye.

At first, I thought I'd just keep walking, keep going up the stairs, that I'd seen a bird or something outside. But then my brain put the dots together, and an image formed of what I'd seen.

It was a group of people walking.

As I went back to the window and looked out, I saw that they were strolling side-by-side, somber body language written all over them. Heads down, shoulders slumped, arms tight to their sides. It was as though they were leaving a funeral. What struck me as even stranger than seeing the group was that I knew who they were.

I recognized every single one of them.

In the back row was my grandpa.

He was supported by my uncle, his right leg incapable of holding his weight. In the front row were my sisters, and *Her*. From this distance she looked to be saddest of all, my older sister keeping an arm around her shoulders in a supportive hug.

"Wait!" I called out, though I knew they couldn't hear me.

"Please, I need you," I said, softer.

I opened my mouth to speak again, but stopped when they disappeared over the horizon, leaving only the green shrubbery that marked where the car had been previously.

It didn't make sense that these people who I knew and loved would be so close, only to leave without even seeing me. Why? I wanted to scream at the top of my lungs in the hopes that they'd hear me, but I knew it was fruitless.

Wiping some tears from my eyes, I experienced another time-glitch, one that left me just as confused as all the rest.

In the few seconds it had taken me to wipe the tears away, snow had fallen, blanketing the landscape in white. Oddly, I could see footprints, seemingly from my family.

A deep wrenching ache, coupled with a sense of longing, came over me as I thought about them and why I was here.

I missed them.

No matter what this strange place was, or why'd I come to begin with, the only thing that I knew for certain was that I felt very alone.

I could only think of two other times I'd ever felt that alone.

*

The first time was during the period of my life when I didn't want to live. My family, in conjunction with my doctor, had checked me into a psychiatric ward at a hospital two hours away. They called it 'a test run,' to see if the next week of intensive treatment, with one-on-one therapy, would jump start the positive side of my brain and push my depression down. I was so angry at this decision, that on the drive there, I punched the roof of the family minivan, knocking the plastic light box out of its socket. As it hung there by the two wires that powered it, swinging back and forth from the motion of the vehicle, I felt abandoned. Obviously, my parents didn't want me around, or so my young, immature, and selfish thoughts preached to my subconscious. When we arrived, I was shown around briefly, as it was getting late, and discovered that I was the youngest person there by a wide margin. I also found out that we had to share a room with another person.

Great.

I've always had trouble sleeping, and during this particular time of my life, I could only fall asleep with the aid of music. I'd press play on my Discman, pull the headphones over my ears, and focus on whatever music was helping me drift off to dreamland. During that time, it was a compilation called "Ocean Waves and Soothing Water Sounds."

Surprisingly, it always worked like a charm.

I'd have the volume low, and sure enough the lapping waves, bird calls, and the swooshing water would relax me. I'd fall into a deep sleep, one that pills could never replicate.

That first night was tough.

My roommate was a forty-five-year-old-male with schizophrenia. Most of the time it was of the paranoid variety. He appeared friendly but was very Neanderthal-like, with a strong jaw, hunched shoulders, and some of the hairiest forearms I've ever seen. I never did find out his name. He might have told me. I just didn't remember. In the short time I was there, he was cordial and encouraging in the group setting. I really hit it off with two other patients. The first was a thirty-something guy named Ed, who told me he had broken under the pressure of his hours being cut at work. His young kids were having some medical difficulties, and then he'd found out his wife had been cheating on him with his brother. He'd snapped at a birthday party, been restrained, and spouted a few sentences that the police deemed unfit. So, he was sent there to be evaluated. We got along great, and chatted for hours about music, cars, women, sports, and our struggles. Ed wasn't very forthcoming when we did group sessions, and he worried out loud to me that because he didn't want to open up to the group, it would hurt his chances of leaving.

The second person I befriended was Juliet.

She was a fifty-five-year-old mother of three, and grandmother of five. When I first met her, I thought she was in her late thirties, so when she told me her age, I was shocked. After her husband of thirty-five years had cleaned out their bank accounts and left her, she'd tried to burn herself alive. This was evident by the heavy scars on the right side of her face and along her right arm. Whenever she sat anywhere, she'd do so in a way that hid that side. She was ashamed of what she'd done, and after finishing her recovery and rehab, she'd been transferred to the psych wing to determine if she was still a danger to herself.

The first three days I was there, we talked frequently, and on each of those days, one of her daughters came by for a visit. Juliet would light up, and to see the joy in her face when her grandkids came running up to her, yelling, 'Grandma, grandma,' was heart-warming. When they brought our morning dose of pills on day four, she refused to take them.

"I'm ready to go home," she defiantly told them.

With that proclamation, the nurses ushered her to her room, where she would wait for the doctor on his rounds, and they'd discuss her decision. I knew it wouldn't be an immediate thing.

If the doctor decided she was fit to leave, then a discharge plan would be implemented. When she refused to take her pills, Ed had leaned in close and said, "I heard a rumor that she's been here for over five years, and none of the nurses think she'll ever leave."

I couldn't fathom that.

Juliet, this kind, amazing person, who'd given me a few spectacular pieces of advice already, would never leave? It just didn't add up.

That afternoon, I had my second one-on-one with the doctor. He was pleasant enough, and younger, around forty or so, and he approached our sessions as though we'd been buddies growing up. I didn't mind this approach, but at times also found it a little off putting.

"So, why're you here? I look at you, and I'm confused. Before me, I see a young, smart, athletic guy, with a loving family. Here you are, surrounded by societies lost and forgotten. Is this where you see yourself ending up? Here, or in the funeral home?"

Blunt.

Nobody had been this straightforward with me yet, and this approach was refreshing. But his statement also startled me. I didn't know how to respond.

"No."

I answered, with no confidence in my response. I expected him to reply with frustration. Instead, he laughed.

"Tell you what. Since you sound so unsure, I've spoken with your family, and we've decided that you'll be here until next Wednesday. You'll be discharged on that day, and they'll be here to take you home. But only if that's what you want. When Wednesday rolls around, and you want to stay, then no problem, we'll admit you for the rest of the month and re-evaluate. Sound fair?"

I sat, staring at the wall behind the doctor, trying not to react. I hadn't expected him to say that. I thought for sure I'd only be there for the week and then get on with my life. Now, here I was, essentially trapped for another week. To make matters worse, if they didn't like my progress, I'd be staying until the end of the month.

"Alright," I stammered. I went back to my room, put my headphones on, and turned on some music. As I closed my eyes, tears rolled down my cheeks.

To this day, I don't know why that moment profoundly moved me the way it did, but it set things in motion, internally, at least, that pushed me forward.

I had a new resolve.

I was better than that place.

I was better than depression.

Little did I know, that while I listened to my music, something had happened on the other side of the ward. It was going to walk up and smack me in my face, giving me an even bigger wake up call.

17.

The next morning, I woke up groggy and disoriented, but aware of a lot of activity in the hallway. I was surprised I'd slept so long. The frustrating news the doctor had delivered the day before danced in my mind, but I pushed it aside as the noise from the hallway increased in volume. If I didn't know any better, I'd have assumed there was a swarm of bees on the other side of the door, but the more I listened, the more I understood it was just everyone talking over one another.

Did I miss a memo? Was there an event today that I'd forgotten?

My roommate was already gone, his bed haphazardly made. Looking over at his cubby, which was supposed to be *our* cubbies, I saw his Velcro running shoes were gone.

I got dressed, brushed my teeth, and left to see what the commotion was.

Everyone was crying.

Even Ed had tears in his eyes when I went over to him, and once he saw me approaching, he wiped them away with his shirt sleeve.

"What's going on?"

"Man..."

He started to say something, but couldn't finish, more tears coming as he choked up.

"Juliet... she uh, she killed herself last night."

The words physically hurt.

My face went numb, and my vision blurred. The room started to spin. I was dizzy, saddened, and very, very confused. The urge to puke snuck up, my eyes seeking the nearest washroom in case I couldn't stop it from happening.

How? How had this happened?

Thinking about it again, the double meaning of what she'd said replayed in my head. She didn't mean go *home*. She never meant to leave this place. She meant to leave on her own terms, and to stop the pain she was in forever.

"Why?" I finally blurted out, the word coming out heavy.

"I don't know. It doesn't make sense. It's just... awful." He let out a sob and another patient wrapped him in an embrace.

Not knowing what else to do, I returned to my room. Music not only helped calm me, but also helped me escape. I wasn't sure how to process the news. It was, at least from my interactions with Juliet, so unexpected. I knew a group session would be inevitable, and assumed that once the administrative aspects were wrapped up, we'd be told when to meet. I figured the longer I stayed in my room, the less I had to be out *there*, near everyone.

I needed to get out as soon as I could, and at the next meeting with the doctor, I would politely ask first, and then beg, if necessary.

Not long after, a nurse came by and let me know that a group meeting would happen in thirty minutes. This one was different from the previous ones. The meeting was slow. Very little was said. The atmosphere was sombre. Most of those who attended stayed quiet while they dabbed their eyes with tissues. I didn't participate much, and when it came time for me to share how I was feeling, I simply said, "Alone."

After the group meeting ended, I went to the doctor's office for our previously scheduled one-on-one. Whether it was because of what had happened with Juliet, or whether I was making strides, this meeting had a very different tone from the one previously. I was more forthcoming. I told him how I've felt alone for most of my life. Growing up in a small town in the middle of nowhere, I felt isolated. As though there was this whole, big world out there that I couldn't access. School was no different. In elementary and middle school, I had friends, but often I was the only boy in my grade.

I played on our school's sports teams and excelled, but once the game or practice would end, I'd return home to be on my own again. Usually, I'd head outside with a ball and a stick and take slapshot after slapshot against one of our garages. Or, I'd grab a stack of hockey cards and flip through them, reading every stat line on the back.

The doctor listened intently and understood where I was coming from, but then he countered with a question of his own.

"Why now?"

What was it about my life, at this moment, that had made it so I wasn't wanting to go on?

I couldn't answer. Not then, and to be honest, I wouldn't have an answer for another year. There was something that had made me hang on, and by hanging on, at the precipice of that void that threatened to swallow me whole, I finally met *Her,* and found a reason to carry on.

When I couldn't answer, the doctor suggested we end the session there and let me know that he was happy with my progress. Our next session was Friday, and we'd discuss our options then.

I was optimistic. I also felt I'd made progress, and accepted that if I needed to spend more time here, then so be it.

Back in my room, I flopped onto the bed and put on some music. Positioning my headphones so they wouldn't irritate my ears, I realized this place wasn't half bad. Maybe it *was* best for me to be there. It was then that I decided another week's stay would be for the best.

My parents came to visit on the weekend, and we went out for some lunch, which felt like an adventure, after having been in the confines of the ward for all that time. We had access to an outdoor area with tables, lawn chairs and some grass, but we seldom spent any time out there.

The following week was one of personal discovery.

Moving in a positive direction was an accurate way to describe it.

The doctor and I kept our conversation going and discussed how I felt, and we worked on some ways for me to process those emotions. We went through coping strategies and when to implement them, as well as how I could identify any negative spiraling that might be occurring.

It was filling me with confidence that I could succeed when I was no longer in that environment. But I won't lie. There was hesitation about leaving, about being alone again, and because of that, I understood why some people end up being institutionalized for life.

Like Juliet.

When Saturday arrived, I was anticipating that it might be the day I would be told I could leave. I wanted to go home, return to school, and try to figure out what my 'new normal' looked like.

After breakfast, I was summoned into the doctor's office and sat across from him. It was an old, brown leather chair that looked like it would be comfortable, but was the furthest thing from that. After the normal pleasantries, he got down the meat and potatoes of our meeting.

"So, do you think you're ready to leave? Are you ready to return to school?"

"I think I am," I replied, knowing full well that he'd pounce on how unconfident I sounded.

"Kids are mean. They can be extremely cruel. They'll talk about your absence, both to your face and behind your back. Are you ready to deal with that?"

"Yes," I said, forcing strength into each letter of the word.

I watched him write down a half dozen sentences on the notepad in front of him, just far enough away that I couldn't make out any of the words.

"I know you've made solid progress over the last week, but I won't let you leave if it means I'll be reading your obituary in a week."

Valid and to the point.

I knew this wasn't his first rodeo. And I knew he was speaking from a place of care, where he wanted to see me succeed. How many teenagers had he dealt with before? Probably less than a handful. Where I grew up, depression wasn't a thing that was spoken about, wasn't something I'd even heard other kids my age have to deal with.

I wanted to tell him that I wouldn't do that, that I was ready to face the world head on, but he spoke first.

"How about this? Take the rest of today and tomorrow morning to think on what awaits you. Then, tomorrow afternoon, we can meet, and if we both agree that you're ready to tackle this next test, I'll call your parents to have them pick you up. But – if I'm not satisfied when we meet, we'll put in a plan for us to work together more frequently and we'll re-evaluate your stay here every two days. How's that sound?"

"*Like horseshit,*" was how I wanted to reply, but I didn't. And I didn't because I couldn't argue with his logic. No matter how much I wanted to leave and go home, have my own room again or even just plead my case to the doctor about letting me out, I knew it wouldn't matter. He made the decision, not me and he'd deftly put the onus back on me. And rightly so. I was the one who needed to make permanent, positive changes.

Especially if I was to make it anywhere in life. Otherwise, I could expect my permanent address to be right where I was.

Or six feet under.

I spent the rest of the day deep in thought. I ate lunch and dinner alone. I told the few folks who approached that I simply wasn't in the mood to visit, and they went on their way. They understood.

The next morning, I was up at the crack of dawn, anxious but hopeful. I was practically vibrating with excitement when I was finally summoned to our appointment. He quickly put my nerves at ease, letting me know he was proud of how far I'd come since arriving, and that he'd called my parents to pick me up. Before I left his office, he shook my hand and said, "I better not see you here again."

Packing my stuff was surreal. A part of me wasn't convinced I was leaving. Would I get to the door, and they wouldn't let me out? It was far more emotional saying goodbye to the few friends I'd made there, surprised at how much I'd come to care for them in such a short time. At the ward doors, two nurses wished me well, and as I walked from the hospital and across the parking lot to where my parents were parked, I felt a weight leave me.

I'd been very angry when I'd been taken there, but now, even though it had been a short stay, I knew it'd been for the best.

As I piled into the back of the vehicle and we drove away, I took one long look back.

It was odd, seeing the building from that perspective. It looked sterile and unwelcoming, whereas, inside the ward, it had felt a cozy and safe place. I realized that I'd spent time with some people I'd never see again. Folks who I'd connected with in a meaningful way, but outside of those walls, our paths would never cross again. On the flip side, there was excitement and trepidation with my departure. Friends I couldn't wait to see and things I desperately wanted to do. And there was a part of me that was happy I was alive.

But truthfully, as we pulled away, there was still that feeling that I'd always be alone.

I'll forever be thankful for that doctor and how he helped me find that tiny sliver of light in my life that I've grown to love. I never remained in touch with any of the other people I met while there. I do hope Ed became everything he wanted and reunited with his kids.

A few years later, while completing some personal growth exercises, I returned for a visit. I wanted to see it one last time and get some closure. That was an odd experience, one that suggested my memories of my time there weren't as complete as I'd thought they were. But the closure of returning and confronting some of those memories was exactly what I needed.

*

The snow-covered field that stretched as far as I could see reinforced how alone I was at that very moment.

I knew that if I didn't figure out what the source of the sound was, or even why my body kept failing, I was going to go insane.

18.

The feeling of things happening but not actually happening made me believe this was a dream. At least what was occurring at that exact moment felt like a dream.

Everything was dark. At first, I was unsure where I even was, but when I shifted, I felt the familiar cushioning of the driver's seat of my car, followed quickly by the digging in of the seatbelt across my chest. The darkness beyond the windshield was unsettling, as though the car was in a room painted the darkest shade of black. I tried to unbuckle the seatbelt, but it wouldn't unclick, no matter how desperately I jammed the button down. Frantically grabbing the door handle, it wouldn't open, even when I could see the locks were clicked up. Outside, a sudden light source illuminated the area directly in front of the car. I could lean forward just enough to see that I was parked beside a very tall building with a light shining from the very top.

I tried to unclip the belt again, but it wasn't cooperating. Something caught my attention while I looked around for a way to cut myself free of the belt. In the distance a large, shadowed figure was moving, snaking through the blackness.

As it closed in, I tried to get the seatbelt off, but with each attempt the belt tightened across my chest, forcing the remaining oxygen in my lungs out. My eyes flickered from the buckle to the creature that moved ever closer. From behind it, a larger shadow loomed, and I realized that it was pulling a massive wave behind it, which was growing larger and larger with each passing second.

As my last breath escaped my lungs, the beast arrived, and with it the tidal wave crashed over me, blocking out the light that shone from the building.

The impact of the water slamming down on the car was like nothing I'd ever felt, battering the vehicle around as though weightless. The frame was no match for the strength of the water, the roof ripping from the body, the water wrapping around me in an instant. As my eyes bulged, the seat was torn away, the bolts no match for the force of the wave. I was still strapped into the seat, which left me defenseless and thrown about like a sock in a washing machine. I could feel every bone in my body being crushed, every muscle being pulled from their attachment points. At the same time, the very real knowledge that I'd drown before my injuries killed me brought panic, and through the watery abyss loved ones and former pets swam to me as their way of sending me off into the great unknown.

First, my grandmother swam over, and I remembered how we watched Saturday morning wrestling together. How she loved to cheer against whichever wrestler I was rooting for in each match. She loved game shows, playing cards, and making fun of my sisters and I when we walked by my grandparent's house on our way home from school. She swam right up to me, pushing the water aside, to give me a kiss on the cheek. Then she pinched it before floating away and disappearing in the darkened waters.

Next, my other dog, OJ galloped over, sneezing as he always did, murky bubbles floating up through the water. He put his front paws on my thighs and began excessively licking my face and ears, even nibbling my earlobe like he always did. I remembered how, when we first adopted him, he'd accidentally ingested one of my earrings doing just that. I felt a tear start down my cheek before it was washed away. How I missed that blockhead, and when he swam away, I let out a sob, gulping in more water.

Then one of my best friends, Pat, appeared. He made a comment about the week of epic bonding we had, years before, when he'd swapped an engine out of my car and put a new one in. We'd worked on it from sunup to sundown, and by work on it I mean Pat did the mechanical stuff and I handed him the tools. When we'd finally got the engine to turn on, you would've sworn we were landing on the moon. We yelled, we shouted, we jumped and high-fived.

Even though my eyes were bathed in tears, I could see the big grin on his face. Slowly he drifted away as another friend formed within the water. Simon. It was nice to see Simon. We'd met through sport, and developed a lifelong friendship, remaining close even as the miles grew further between us. I remembered the Christmas dinner he'd attended at our place, and how he complained that there was no surf and turf available, just turkey. He patted my shoulder and mouthed, "*Take care old friend*," as he dissolved within a flurry of bubbles.

Then came Jody.

He grabbed my bicep and squeezed, before wrapping his arms around me in a hug. We'd done a bunch of ridiculous things together over the years. I remembered the first time we really chatted at a Foot Locker in the local mall, soon after becoming friends. The memory that really stuck out was when he invited me over to his shop so I could meet a brown bear. The bear was trained for movies, which made for some great photo ops. We'd been a constant in each other's lives for almost two decades, as he became a lot like the older brother I never had. "*Gonna miss you, bro,*" he said, as he let go and drifted away towards the surface.

Once he disappeared, the reality of my drowning took over, the lack of oxygen slamming into my chest and brain with the force of a million punches. The only reason I was still alive was so that the apparitions of my friends and family had time to say their goodbyes.

Finally, my grandpa swam over, and in his hands was my first dog, Jake.

He set Jake on my lap, who licked my face, and then curled into a ball. My grandpa gave me a hug, while I tried to pet Jake, but my hands wouldn't respond.

You need to wake up, I told myself. *This is a distraction.*

Even though I was underwater, I could feel the sweat thicken on my forehead and run down my back. A hotness took hold, a burning from deep inside, deeper than the pain in my lungs. My grandpa, sensing a change in me, picked up Jake, and began to float away. As he did this, the seatbelt tightened once more, cutting off the circulation in my lower body. My legs went numb and ballooned. A huge roar went through the water, followed by a giant wave crashing down on me, sending the seat, and myself, careening through the water. With one more giant rush, I was flung high from the water, soaring through the air, before slamming onto the sandy beach at the shore.

The seat landed on an angle with me facing away from the water. The back section of the seat had dug into the sand. I could feel the water lap at my heels as wave after wave washed onto the shore. I tried to shift forward, but the seat wouldn't budge, the sand holding fast. I tried to rock forward again, but as I did, the sand around me sloughed away and I toppled backwards, falling to the ground. I was stuck and was carried with the chair as it fell backwards.

Laying there, trapped, my face turned red, the seatbelt so tight that it was choking me. A sob tried to form deep in my throat, but it was no use. I was unable to make any sort of noise. My vision blurred, but through the haze, I could see a figure approaching. Once it was next to me, I shuddered, seeing that it was the shadowed figure who'd brought the wave down upon me in the first place. It reached over, and pulled the belt tighter, crushing my diaphragm and stomach, and splintering my vertebrae. My body was paralyzed and numb. The total loss of sensation should have rattled me, but it didn't. To my surprise I saw the water flow away, and with it my lower body too. The seatbelt had cut me in half.

I tried to scream for my legs to come back, but as I opened my mouth, blood poured out, turning the water into a kaleidoscope of blue and red.

"Your pain is ending," the figure said to me. "You can wake up now. It's time."

*

I was jolted awake.

My clothes were drenched, and I wondered if it's from sweat or the dream. Quickly, I reached down to feel for my legs, and breathed a sigh of relief when I felt them still attached to my body. Looking around, I found that I wasn't on a beach, and there was no sign of the car seat.

The neon brightness of the coolers illuminated the area around me, and I remembered that I was at the gas station, still behind the counter. I didn't see the woman anywhere, nor did I hear her, but the light of dawn shining through the window filled me with a sensation bordering on hope. *Maybe, just maybe, that monsters moved on.*

I was back in the gas station, behind the counter.

Getting to my knees, I peered over the counter, glad to see that the front door hadn't been bashed down. I sensed a presence from the back of the store, but that may have been my paranoia.

"Hello?"

I spoke quietly, afraid to alert whatever may be waiting outside for me, but it was enough that the door to the stock room opened, and the woman appeared.

"Is it gone?"

"It left not long after you fell asleep," she said. "Glad you woke up, though. I was starting to worry you were going to sleep forever."

I wanted to believe her, that the *thing* had left, but I needed to see for myself, so I went to the edge of the large exterior window and looked out, finding nothing but the barren gas pumps and the strip of dirt that ran alongside the highway.

"Did you get it to leave?" I asked.

"Ha!"

In the stillness of the gas station the sound surprised me.

This was not the response I expected, but the lightness in her reply helped to reduce how on edge I was.

"Well, whatever that thing is that was looking for you, it tried real hard to get in. I was able to activate the maglock on the doors, so it couldn't. It tried a few times, slamming into the glass, and I thought it was going to break through, but then it just stopped and left. You didn't even flinch."

The glass on the front door showed signs of being hit, but there wasn't a crack to be found. Through it, I could see my car was still parked by the gas pumps. The car brought back the emotions of my dream, but the dream had already started to fade. All I could remember were sadness and goodbyes.

"I think I should be getting on," I said. "I'd like to make it to Edgewater today if possible."

She came and placed a hand on my shoulder.

"You won't make it to Edgewater tonight. Maybe tomorrow."

She handed me the bag with the sandwich and drink, which I'd forgotten about, and told me to eat it first before getting gas. Sitting on a chair at the counter, I ate it in four bites with a hunger I'd never felt before.

I said my goodbyes and thanked her again, as she went behind the counter and flipped the gas pump on. I watched as she grabbed the bucket and squeegee and returned to cleaning the coolers.

Without another word I stepped out into the early morning sunshine, the understanding that I'd never see her again settling like a fog.

No birds chirped, nor could I hear any cars. An eerie calmness had a hold of the world. At the car, I opened the passenger door and tossed the bag of snacks on the floor. Closing the door, I opened the gas hatch and undid the cap, sliding the nozzle in. As I gripped the handle and the sound of the gas pumping began, a smell arrived. At first, I thought that maybe it was the gas. Maybe it'd been sitting for long enough to go bad. Did gas even go bad? I had no idea if it did, and if so, if the smell would change. A slight breeze picked up and with it, the smell increased, forcing me to cough. While doing so, my attention returned to the gas station and when my eyes fell upon it, my jaw dropped.

The gas station looked as though it'd been closed for years.

The large window had a thick crack running across it, the glass itself covered in mildew and grime. The front door had a 'closed' sign on it that hung on an angle from a single string, the other side broken and dangling. I holstered the nozzle and screwed the gas cap closed.

Flipping the hatch shut, I tentatively approached the station. I tried to open the front door, but it wouldn't budge. Through the smeared glass, I could see the handles on the inside had thick chains wrapped throughout them, a big lock clasped to keep it shut. Going to the big window, I cupped my face so that I could look through, and felt my heart drop when I saw the barren interior. The coolers were dark and empty. The shelves were devoid of product, and over in the far corner I could see a discarded red bucket, the same one that woman had been using to clean with.

Unable to trust that I wouldn't puke, I stumbled back towards the car, but stopped when I saw the truck. When I'd pulled in the night before, there'd been a 1970's style Ford truck, with side steps behind the cab. It had been in immaculate condition, something the owner took great pride in.

Now, it was a rusting thing forgotten by whomever loved it.

All four tires were flat, and the windows were covered in a thick layer of dust. The driver's side mirror was hanging beside the body. Whether it'd fallen off or been broken, I couldn't tell.

A gust of wind came, a noise behind me spinning me around to look at the store once again. A sign was taped to the large window, which didn't make sense. I'd not seen it but knew there was no way I would've missed it.

To our valued customers. Due to the slowdown, we're closing. Sorry for the inconvenience. We've appreciated your loyalty all these years. Management. Frank's Grocery and Gas – 1948-1960.

1960.

How was that possible? My head spun.

I ran to the front door and tried it again, but it still wouldn't move. I slammed my fists against it, desperately wanting to see the woman appear from the back room, but she didn't.

Dread took over.

LEAVE, NOW, a voice yelled from inside my head.

I listened.

Running to the car, I climbed in, but paused when I grabbed the seatbelt, the dream flooding my brain for half a second. Ignoring it, I clicked the belt closed and turned the car on, relieved to see the gas gauge indicate it was full. Seeing as how the gas station had magically aged while I filled up, it wouldn't've surprised me if no gas had been pumped. But the gauge said otherwise, and that was good enough for me. At the edge of the dirt strip, I stopped and looked both ways before entering the road, even though I knew there weren't going to be any cars.

As I left, I looked in the mirror once more, but instead of the gas station reflecting back, all that I saw was an empty lot. Looking at the road ahead, I saw the young woman standing on the side of the road. I gave the horn a light honk and waved. As I drove past her, she faded into the mist, disappearing before my very eyes.

With that, snow began to fall again, and I put my thoughts ahead to Edgewater.

She'd said I wouldn't arrive today, but maybe she was wrong? Or was I never to reach my destination? Was I trapped in an infinite loop? One where a beast was pursuing me and time had its own rules?

The road ahead was curved, short lefts and rights, but I kept the speed controlled, not wanting a repeat of my previous white-knuckle experiences. The snow was falling harder, accumulating on the shoulder, and further down the highway I could see the pavement had started to hold some of the whiteness.

A straight section came after the last short corner, which let me relax a bit. Halfway across the span, I could see a road sign, so I slowed and pulled to a stop near it. The snowfall had increased, making most the sign illegible. I climbed from the car and wiped the sign clear with my sleeve, and felt my world crash around me as the words came into view.

Summit 5, Fuel 50, Edgewater 250.

19.

Have you ever read a book where the main character arrives at a moment of extreme insanity, and we see their mind crack? Rarely does that occur in the real world, but at that exact second, I knew my mind was about to crumble into a million pieces. I could feel my knees turn to rubber, my midsection a mass of gel, sloppy and slimy.

The words on that sign...

I stood, trying to process what in the hell I was reading. It simply didn't make sense. I'd driven hundreds of miles. It'd been several days. And yet... and yet, somehow the sign I was parked beside had the exact same mileage on it as that blasted sign that I'd found covered in leaves and debris.

I'd experienced so many moments of sheer confusion over the last few days that I should've been able to handle whatever the next crazy thing was. But apparently, I wasn't.

Standing on the side of the road, my brain began to tell me lies. That this straight stretch was the same as the previous one. That I'd not been at the gas station, it had only been a dream. That I was at back home, dreaming this while I napped on the couch. I knew this was all untrue, but my mind was really pushing hard with these falsehoods, which I started to understand were just another step down the road to total and complete insanity. I'd already lost it, but this was the official point where there was no coming back from. The deep end.

The sun appeared over the snow-capped peaks around the area, wind whipping through the windy ravines and blasting across the open space where I was. I should've got back in the car, but for just a second, the feeling of the wind battering my skin let me know I was alive, that this *was* happening, no matter what my brain suggested.

Rereading the sign, I had the urge to punch the green metal, but knew that it would do nothing but break my hand and cause me unnecessary pain. And that had been the one constant since I drove away from everything – pain. There was no need to invite more into my life. There'd be more soon enough.

Climbing back into the car, I opened and closed my hands, the cold having numbed my fingers. Even with the heat cranked on full blast, my fingers refused to get any feeling back into them. The wind slammed into the side of the car while I was shaking my hands in an attempt to get the circulation moving. It hit with such force that I was rocked into the door, my head striking the window. I shook my head, not because there was pain, but because my vision went double for a split second. But in doing so, I noticed that the forest was closing in, a darkness pushing the trees across the open field.

As I watched the trees dig through the dirt, my neck turned to granite, unable to turn, my eyes locked on the blackness encroaching. My breath hitched in my throat, a weight pushing on my body. Sitting there, I focused on the snow that was accumulating on the hood and windshield of the car. If I was to keep watching the trees I knew I'd start screaming and wouldn't be able to stop. Madness existed and it was changing the landscape before my very eyes.

A wave of nausea slid through me, my neck loosening as my stomach clenched. I closed my eyes and opened them, hoping beyond hope that the sign might've changed, or that the trees had stopped, but neither had occurred.

"Why is this happening?" I shouted at the top of my lungs alone in the car, hammering my still numb hands again and again on the steering wheel. For a moment I thought I was hitting the wheel so hard that the car was moving, but when I stopped, I realized that the mountains had started to tremble and shake, the trees rocking back and forth as though a huge wind was blowing them as it pleased. I wanted to throw the car into reverse and leave, head back towards the gas station and the beast. But, as I gripped the wheel and watched, the black shadow that had been behind the trees pushed through and I knew that the beast had caught up.

I slid the lever into drive and slammed the gas pedal, the car lurching forward and accelerating away from the shapeless creature that lunged towards me. I saw the outline of claws swipe inches from the driver side mirror, and then I was past, zooming away through the snow, away from the void that had crashed down where I'd been parked.

As I rounded the corner and drove back into the winding roads of the mountains, I broke down.

The tears came and I couldn't stop them. It was futile. This. Me. Everything. I wished I could be free of this hell, get through it and put it all behind me, but no matter how far I tried to get away, there it was. Always right where I was, always waiting.

My thoughts turned to *Her*.

Her love. Her anger. Her disappointment. Her fear.

She'd never understand my decision, but I knew she would've always been there for me. But I couldn't let that happen. She didn't deserve what the future would bring. She deserved the world and more.

The wipers struggled to keep the snow off, failing as the flakes increased in size and volume.

Driving along, cruising down some nameless highway, I wondered when this would come to an end. Would it be me that decided that? Or would the giant, apocalyptic beast finally catch up and devour what was left of me?

The longer I drove, the sadder my thoughts turned. No matter how much I tried to think of something happy, my brain went down a different path, filling me with sorrow. I was hungry, exhausted, and devoid of hope. I just wanted this chaos to end. But it seemed as though I'd be driving forever, stuck on this highway that went nowhere.

Then, as I looped around a slight left and pitched up and over a low rise, the view before me changed almost instantly. Gone were the hills and peaks of the mountains and beyond that were shorter trees and longer fields. It was subtle but welcomed. I felt safer. I could see more of the land around me, and the snow had thinned. Along the stretch, several smaller pullouts appeared, but I didn't want a repeat of the previous mountain top experience, so I continued, hoping that I'd managed to lessen the distance to Edgewater. I knew I'd need to sleep soon; my eyes were starting to feel heavy, but I couldn't stop now.

If a house or hotel or anything resembling a place I could sleep didn't appear within the next thirty minutes, I decided I'd pull over and sleep for an hour. The thought sent ripples of fear through me, knowing I'd be exposed with nothing to warn me if my pursuer approached, but it was either that or potentially fall asleep, which I didn't want to do while driving.

It had been years since I'd been this tired. I wasn't a teenage boy anymore; I couldn't stay up all night playing video games and then be productive the following day. I needed sleep, and I needed it soon.

The road weaved gently, almost hypnotically, as I drove. Ahead, a short rise met me, and just over it, a long, straight stretch. Even though it was devoid of any structures, the sight of how open everything was filled me with glee. This was a perfect place to stop.

Stopping the car in the middle of the pullout, I eased my way out, then stood and stretched, letting out a comically loud yawn while I scratched my bare belly where my shirt and coat had risen up.

Looking around, I knew this was a solid place to sleep. I was far from the hills that loomed in the distance, making it so that no beast could surprise me with an unseen ambush. The snow had all but stopped, and while the dirt was crunchy from the ice, it wasn't slippery. If I needed to make a hasty getaway, it'd be possible.

Circling around the car, I breathed in the refreshing, crisp air. As much as I wanted to crawl into the back seat and go to sleep, being out of the car and walking felt reinvigorating. I could still feel the heaviness of sleep deprivation wanting to take hold, but the cold air and exercising my muscles kept it at bay.

Two more short loops around the car later, I flipped the driver seat forward, crawled into the back of the car, and flopped onto the back seat. I leaned over and closed the door, making sure to engage the locks. Using my sweatshirt, I rolled it up to make a pillow for myself and then wiggled around, getting into a comfortable enough position across the back seat of the car. I had to shift a few times until I got things right, and as I did, I took a deep breath of the sweatshirt and sat up, looking at it.

Her.

It smelled like *Her.*

Had she worn it last? I thought I'd worn it on the drive? It didn't matter. I jammed my nose into the material, breathing deeply, even as tears began to flow. The reality of what was happening hit hard. My arms would never be strong enough to hold her again. My legs would never be able to dance with her again. The muscles in my face would never let me smile at her again. And so, I'd fled. I'd packed a few things in my pack and took off on this foolish, asinine adventure.

Adventure?

Was this supposed to be some huge, cataclysmic experience, changing me forever?

It seemed to be anything but that. There were no positives coming from this trip, and the only thing it was doing was reminding me how far down the road I'd gone, and just how much I missed *Her*. It physically hurt.

But there was nothing I could do about that. I was exhausted, filled with regrets, and with no way of turning back the clock. So, I allowed my body to succumb, and fell asleep with my nose buried deep into that sweatshirt.

*

The dream started instantly.

The first thing I saw was the road ahead, but it wasn't the highway I'd been driving on. No, this was familiar. I couldn't say for certain, but I had the sense that I was driving towards the college I'd attended. The edges of my peripheral vision were fuzzy, suggesting this was a dream, even within the dream. A different sort of feeling than how my tired brain had been processing things before I'd fallen asleep. A familiar song played, one that brought me back to the summer before grade nine. I'd spent every waking minute with my best friend. We were a pair of jokers, interested in only two things – laughing and boobs.

Our days were spent at the beach, hanging with friends, swimming or playing volleyball, and then we'd spend the nights watching cartoons, movies, or playing video games. We'd talk about the future and what we would grow up to do. We had sky high plans with no real idea of how to achieve them.

That summer was one of the best times in my life.

I think back on it often, reliving those carefree days of sun, sand, and friends.

The following summer, we hung again, but not as much as before, and that dropped even more as my depression caused us to drift apart.

We remained acquaintances until I graduated, a year ahead of him.

Some years after I moved away, I ran into him and a few others I'd gone to high school with at a concert. It was cordial at the time, but all it did was remind me of that wonderful summer. That summer we lost a friend, killed by a drunk driver. That summer we camped, we canoed, we swung from rope swings, and we laughed until we couldn't laugh anymore.

Even as the years pass, I wish for those days again, of clear skies and infinite potential.

My attention turned from the song to the person walking along the road ahead. They had on a backpack and a hard hat. They looked my way as I drove, before turning and sticking out their thumb, hoping I'd stop.

Do I know them?

I slowed and stopped just past them, watching in the passenger mirror as they jogged. Once at the car, they thanked me before they were even fully inside. As they got situated, I looked over and saw that this person looked strikingly like a good friend, but their face refused to come into focus.

"Where to, friend?" I asked. Did they recognize me? I was positive I'd met them before.

They started to speak, but stopped, their lips shimmering and vibrating as though made of static.

"Sorry, what was that?"

"I'm not sure," they said. "I can't stay here, but I don't know where to go."

I was equally confused and intrigued.

"Do you live near here?"

"Yes and no."

Knowing that was all I'd get from them, I put the car in drive and continued down the road. *Maybe they were going to kill me?*

I glanced over again, which they noticed.

"Thanks, though, for stopping. Most people won't."

"People are afraid of being stabbed by strangers," I said, hoping they took it as a joke.

They didn't reply, but after another five minutes of silence, I could hear they'd started lightly humming. To my surprise, it was the song that had played earlier, the one that reminded me of that summer all those years ago.

I looked at them again, but their face was still distorted and misshapen.

"Do you know me? Do you remember who I am?"

They kept humming, their body rocking rhythmically to the tune.

I wanted to scream at them to just fucking answer me, but instead they started humming louder, as though working towards a glorious crescendo. Then, at the apex of the song, they abruptly stopped and spoke.

"Do you remember you?"

"I..."

A reply had formed and faded. Memories of who I was were there, but those memories were of someone I no longer recognized.

"You know, she'll always love you. She's gonna miss you forever."

Through the distortion of their face, I could see tears in their eyes, a shallow smile made from sadness.

"I *can't* put Her through this."

They nodded – whether out of pity or agreement, I couldn't tell – and then reached over and put a hand on my shoulder.

"You're loved. By many. But Her love means more than the rest combined. Make it right with *Her*. She's your everything. She deserves that much, at least."

I tried to respond, but nothing came.

As if sensing my inability to speak, they rapped a knuckle on the dash and said, "This looks like as good a place to stop as any. It's been great catching up, and I wish you nothing but the best on this journey. I hope, for your sake, you find what you're looking for. The answers you seek are ahead. Not far. The Lighthouse. That's where your journey comes full circle."

They opened the door and stepped out, before reaching back in to grab the backpack. I watched as they walked down the road, away from the car. Soon, they faded, dissolving from view as though they'd never been there in the first place.

I took a moment and collected my thoughts before continuing. With each mile that zipped past, my peripheral vision grew fuzzier, the dream-state beginning to fade. With an expectation of waking, I was surprised when I saw another figure ahead, this one a woman, and one I recognized immediately.

My aunt.

I stopped the car and clambered out, running around the front to wrap her in a big hug. It'd be almost two decades since I'd last seen her, and I missed her something fierce. I didn't question that she was standing there, knowing this dream was playing a role in whatever was happening in the real world, but that didn't stop this moment from hurting, from reminding me that she wasn't still alive.

"How are you, kiddo?" she asked.

"I can't believe it's you," I said.

"Of course it's me. We've got some things to discuss, and you've got decisions to make."

We climbed back into the car, a surrealness hanging heavy over the interior.

The last time I'd seen her was in the last few days of her life. Cancer had taken her, leaving behind her family. Even in the dream, this was a special moment.

"Are you sure this is what needs to happen?" she asked.

"If I wasn't, then I'd never have driven away," I replied, knowing she'd understand.

"Drive away, then," she said, "And let's talk."

I pulled back onto the highway, accelerating away from the darkness that continued to creep.

XXX.

Heavy thunder rolled across the hills; thick forks of lightning following.

Clouds had formed not long after I'd fallen asleep, a mix of snow and rain arriving a short time after. The storm slid through the valleys and across the fields, finding the car as though guided by a mysterious force.

Another loud boom of thunder sounded, the beast groaning and rolling over where it slept. It moved its body like that of an old animal, its muscles working hard to walk with such an enormous mass upon them. It reached over and used the trunk of a nearby tree as leverage, its thick clawed hands wrapping around the bark as it pulled itself to its full, impressive height.

As it stretched and shook off the last remnants of sleep, its wide snout raised and inhaled the air, processing the thousands of scents that invaded its nostrils.

It was one of those smells that caught its attention, the one odor it was seeking.

Human.

The pungent stench of sweat, oil, fear, exhaustion, and decay swept across the land and excited the beast.

Within that smell it knew what the disgusting, vile creature was going through, and to know that it was the cause of the human's breakdown filled it with immense pleasure.

Again, the thunder rumbled.

The massive flash of lightning that came just after illuminated the forest, fully exposing the creature for the briefest of seconds. Even the trees around it were disturbed by how hideous it was, their branches pulling back, leaves shrinking.

In response to nature's disrespect, the beast flung its giant arms wide, and let out a blood curdling roar. This roar rippled throughout the forest, rattling the trees, and frightening the animals to their cores. They fled, scampering away, seeking safety.

Satisfied that it'd made its point, it sniffed again, processing what the air told it this time. The stench of the human's putrid flesh gave it all the data it would need. It was close. But that didn't mean the beast was going to rush to the man and disembowel him in short order. No, instead, it would take its time. Stalk the man. Let it know it was near, much like it'd done at the gas station.

And when the time was right...

Only then would it launch its assault.

Thunder boomed across the sky. Snow fell high in the hills, rain falling harder in the lowlands.

The beast dropped to all fours and began to walk, moving through the darkness of the woods, its adapted eyes allowing it to see more than most. Off to the right was a mother deer and a fawn. Before the animals knew what was happening, it grabbed the mother around the neck and tossed the fawn into its jaws. The beast crunched the defenseless creature twice and swallowed. Squeezing tight on the mother deer until its bones snapped and its life stopped, the beast carried it for several more steps, before biting its head off. After swallowing, it tossed the body to the side, not yet feeling satiated.

Leaving the beheaded corpse behind, it moved on, following its nose towards its next victim. A clearing ahead was its destination, across it, an immense brown bear. Upon the beast's arrival at the far edge, the bear stood, sensing its present. Close to eleven feet tall on its hind legs, the bear had few challengers, but when it saw the beast, it bellowed and dropped, rushing across the clearing to attack.

The beast watched in humor at the brute's pathetic display, then charged, barreling into the bear with a violent impact. didn't even slow. As they connected, the beast swiped at its midsection, slicing through the thick hide and fat, and ripping its entrails out with ease. It carried across the clearing, crushing the bears skull against a tree and only then did it stop, letting the bear's body flop lifelessly to the forest floor.

Nothing was going to get in the way of the beast.

The human had no idea what was in store.

20.

The arrival of the beast was something I felt before I'd even opened my eyes.

I'd had chaotic dreams, but I couldn't remember a single word that had been spoken.

The plan to set an alarm had failed, as in my exhausted state, I had forgotten. But I'd woken when the sensation of impending doom had engulfed every cell in my body.

Something was on its way, and it'd be here soon.

What should I do?

It was a question I asked myself, but at the same time it brought back parts of another dream. There'd been a Lighthouse. That I was sure of. Something had been off, and there was a feeling that something bad was about to happen. My body had gone numb. Loud noises had sounded. My car... it had been parked, but was being slowly consumed by vegetation.

There was something outside the car. I had watched it move quickly towards where I was standing. As it approached, the shape had formed into that of a massive monster, a beast so repulsive that I'd felt my heart clench and the front of my pants warm. It came faster and faster, my feet not able to move, my body frozen in place. And right before it slammed into the thin veil that separated the dream me from the real me, my subconscious screamed as loudly as it could.

Wake up!

And I did.

I was in the car, the wind howling outside, and with each new flake of snow that fell, the sense of dread increased.

My brain began to unscramble the pieces. That Lighthouse. I'd never been there. That place had been in my dreams, a place I kept returning to each time I fell asleep. It'd felt real, as though I'd been there, as though I was going there. But the truth was I'd never stepped foot there. I never would.

The Lighthouse dreams had been warnings, but my exhaustion had prevented my brain from understanding that.

And I understood that I was about to find out what the cause of that hideous noise in the Lighthouse was.

Because the source of that sound was racing across the field towards me.

21.

In the back of the car, I watched as it came.

I watched as this abomination of nature rushed towards where I sat, death in its eyes. Its long claws churned the dirt below it as it moved, the ground ripped apart from the sheer power of each stride.

I'd never seen anything this large before in my life, at least not something that was alive.

My heart sank.

The time had come.

There was nowhere to hide, no gas station attendant to help me, and at the speed it was travelling, there was no way I could drive away fast enough.

I couldn't outrun it, not this time.

The end. The end was here.

I'd expected to go further.

Instead of sorrow, I felt acceptance.

I swung the door open and stepped out, closing it behind me. As the door clicked shut, I thought of going back for the sweatshirt that smelled of *Her*, but decided against it.

The beast closed in.

So heavy, each of its foot falls rumbled the highway, the car swaying.

Waiting for it, I leaned casually against the hood of the car, crossing my arms. With nowhere to go, there was no need for me to hide. From where I was, I could smell the stench of the beast, the ripe odor arriving just ahead of it.

Once it got to the highway, it slowed, stopping a dozen feet from me.

"What do you want?" I shouted at the beast. I was angry. I knew I had no hope of surviving, but I still wanted to try to prolong my time.

It didn't reply, just stood there on all fours, thick strands of drool leaking from its clenched jaws. The blood-stained tips of each fang protruded from between its black lips. I could see its nostrils flare, the brow lower as it sized me up.

The wind blew from east to west, but everything else had paused, the world around us keeping its distance.

"What are you waiting for!"

I closed my eyes, expecting it to lunge and rip me limb from limb.

When nothing happened, I opened my eyes, finding the beast only an inch from my face. As our eyes met, it breathed out, its muscles tensing.

"Are you ready?" With a voice like gravel being put through a blender, it asked a question so loaded, I wasn't sure how to respond.

No, I wasn't. Of course not. But also yes, I was. I knew this was what needed to happen.

"Well? Are you as weak in your mind as you are of body?"

"Fuck. You."

I said it defiantly, wanting to show this beast that I was not scared, but it didn't matter. It answered with violence, lashing out towards me, grabbing me by the legs and swinging me through the air, slamming me with such thunderous force on the highway that I was ripped in two. Then, my upper half bounced away, my vision showing me the beast back by the car, as I careened down the asphalt.

Pain rocketed throughout what was left of me, my mind surrendering, shock taking over. I came to a stop two-hundred feet from the car, and the beast took two steps towards me before my vision went dark.

THUMP, THUMP.

22.

Blinding light.

That's what came first.

Was I back in the Lighthouse?

Agony.

That came next.

Every inch of my body erupted in agony, my body convulsing as the pain took hold.

I couldn't be back at the Lighthouse. That was a dream. It wasn't real.

My eyes struggled to open, even as I pleaded for it to happen. My body wouldn't respond to my wishes.

Had I gone crazy?

Looking down, I saw I was still ripped in half, though instead of shredded skin and a pool of blood, it looked like I'd been erased. As though an artist wasn't happy with how they drew my legs, and they'd taken an eraser to the pencil lines. I wasn't whole.

Have I ever been?

Something evil was near, that I could tell, but I couldn't get away from it. There I lay, discarded.

THUMP, THUMP.

That godforsaken sound came from close by, a noise that signaled the end of my rational brain.

If I'd had legs, I might have made my last stand, but without them, I could only wait for it to descend upon me. If I were able to go, would I ascend the stairs of the Lighthouse one last time? Would I look out of that window and see my car entangled by vegetation? Would each floor look the same as I remembered? What month would that calendar display?

At the top, would I walk out onto that deck, finding a boat in the bay or broken upon the rocks below?

Or would I flee? Running from this place one last time, running into the distance for as long and as far as I could?

THUMP, THUMP.

The sound was close, as near to me as it had ever been. My eyes fought to open, to look upon the source finally, but instead they only allowed me to squint, the brightness that surrounded where I lay too much for my retinas to take.

A figure approached, a shadow that blocked some of the light. As my eyes adjusted, the smell hit me and I knew without a doubt that what loomed over me is the beast, and that this time, it'll finish the job.

I tried to speak, a single sound about to escape when another smell arrived, and my heart leapt.

Her.

She was here as well. The love of my life.

Thump, thump.

After all this time, the source had revealed itself, and it was the sound of my heart beating against her hand. She'd placed it on my chest, a touch so gentle, but so warm.

The beast moved beside her, but she didn't shift, even as its mass seemed to push her. With a strength I knew she had, she stood her ground, not letting it take an inch.

I wanted to yell to her when the beast reached for her, but I couldn't, my voice too weak. It didn't grab her. Instead, it lay a long, clawed hand over top of hers, both feeling my heart.

"You're strong," the beast said. She made no motion, which told me she couldn't hear or see this monstrosity, but I knew she felt its presence. For as it spoke, her hand felt warmer against my skin. "Far stronger than I ever imagined. But we can only keep our strength for so long before it fails. And I think you know; you've been failing for some time."

I nodded.

A single tear appeared at the corner of my eye, broke free, and streamed down my cheek. She wiped it away with the back of her hand.

"I'm sorry you were chosen," the beast said, and looking at it, I saw it was sincere.

"You've impressed me with your resilience, and because of that, I'm going to extend to you the greatest gift you have... time."

At first, I didn't understand, but then the beast spoke again.

"Since you were diagnosed, I've thrown nothing but challenges at you. Physical and mental. And up until our confrontation on the highway, you've managed them all. This disease has taken everything from you, and as it takes the last thing you have, I want you to say your final goodbyes with those who've not come to you in your visions."

It took my hand, as though she was no longer standing there, and snapped its fingers.

I found myself standing on the deck of the Lighthouse.

23.

From a distance, you'd have thought it was two lifelong friends reminiscing. We stood at the railing, overlooking the sea that shined a blue for as far as the world travelled away.

Up close, it was a different picture.

A man. And the disease that had eaten him from the inside.

I should've relished having legs again, should've danced and jumped and clicked my heels. But I knew it was fleeting, knew it was a mirage. I was somewhere else at that very moment, a body wasted and drained of its strength and essence.

"You've earned this," it said. "Feel the sun. Soak it in. Breathe in that air. This is for you. You've fought as hard as you could. Your loved ones are proud. But now, this part of your journey comes to an end. Follow me."

I watched as it climbed onto the railing and without looking back, leaped, falling towards the water below.

Knowing what I must do, I climbed as well, standing tall with my arms held high. I'd been through so much, but it was time to rest.

Time to go.

I closed my eyes.

I counted to three.

And I jumped.

24.

The beeping of machines was what I heard next.

Not the wind in my ears as I dove from the Lighthouse.

Not the splash of water or the coldness of the sea as I landed.

The beeping of machines. The hiss and pump of what was keeping me alive.

The sun that had shone so brightly upon that deck was the fluorescent lights of the room. The air that I'd breathed so deeply was from the oxygen mask that adorned my face.

A shell of a man. Only alive because of machines but those would soon be shut off.

I couldn't move, couldn't lift my arms or swing my legs over the edge of the bed. When was the last time I'd even taken a step? I felt a weight shift beside me, so I turned my head, the moment of gloom fading as I saw who it was.

My son.

He sat on the bed beside me, my useless left arm draped over his shoulder. He was playing a video game, the device in his hands. I watched him for a moment before my wife noticed I was awake. Once she did, she came over and gave me a kiss, the smell of *Her* reminding me of a rolled-up sweatshirt in the back of a car. My son paused his game, snuggling in closer. I wish this wasn't going to be how he remembered me, but it would be.

If only he could remember what I did.

I remembered the giggle he had as an infant. And how when he started to crawl, his left leg was always far out to the side as though he needed extra balance. How he loved giant monsters and loved to draw them. I remembered how he slept on my chest after he was born, and how I was there for every cold and flu, making sure he understood that I'd always have his back.

Until I no longer could.

Until I began to drop glasses and trip over rocks. And how I couldn't pick him up and my hands developed a tremor. How I forget birthdates and bill payments and the bank card pins.

And when I was diagnosed, my wife cried, and I had to try and explain to my son what that meant.

I'd done everything in my power to teach him what I knew, and to set them up for a lifetime of wonderful memories of me and of us. But those wouldn't be at the front of their minds for some time.

"Ghhhrrtt." I tried to speak, but my vocal cords were too weak, and the oxygen mask blocked most of it.

My son leaned close and hugged me, and I didn't care that it hurt. I needed his hug more than the pain to diminish.

"What is it, dad?"

Fuck, did he sound grown up.

Grown up.

I'd never see that.

Wouldn't see him graduate or get married or have grandkids or buy his first house. I sobbed, a noise that alarmed them, and my wife hit the call button for a nurse or doctor to come.

"What is it, honey?" She came closer and pulled the mask aside just enough so that I managed to whisper some words to her.

"We love you so much," she said, taking my hand in hers. With her other arm, she wiped the tears from her face, before wiping mine as well.

The door to the room opened then, a nurse coming in to speak with my wife.

While this took place, my son put his legs over my lap and pushed his forehead into my neck.

"I'll never forget you, dad. I love you."

It was the last thing he ever said to me, and it was the most perfect thing he'd ever said.

My wife came over as the nurse left the room. She climbed onto the other side of the bed. Across the room, I saw the beast.

Just one more minute, please?

It nodded, which was good enough for me.

There were a million things I wanted to say, but I couldn't. If I had the strength and the ability, I might've, but a part of me knew I'd have been happy to just sit as we were, the three of us, hugging until the end of time.

At least mine.

What would I have said?

I'd have told my wife that she'd be ok. It would take time, but happiness would find her again.

I'd tell my son to follow his dreams. That he could be whatever he wanted, and that the future was his.

I'd tell them that I was sorry.

Sorry for leaving them, sorry for failing them, and sorry that this thing I couldn't control would cause them far more pain than I'd ever experienced.

And I'd tell them that the sun would shine again. Light would find them. And that even on the darkest days, to think of me and know that I was there, watching from afar.

As though sensing all of this and that I had no more to give, my wife pulled our son close and said, "It's ok. You can go now."

I smiled, and, in my mind, I thanked her. Thanked them both.

She paged the nurse again, though everything had become muffled. As my son climbed off, I watched him until he was too blurry to see. The blurriness wasn't from tears, I realized, but from my eyesight fading away.

More people entered the room. Who? I wasn't sure. Doctors and nurses most likely. I could still smell my wife, who approached with another. They spoke and then she leaned in, her smell right above my head. I felt her lips on my forehead one last time, before the distant sounds of the machines that kept me alive ceased.

"It's time," the beast said, its voice as clear as day.

I looked at the creature, finding my vision perfect once more. The silhouette of my wife and another was near him, and I wanted to beg the beast to let me see her one last time, but it shook its head before I could even ask.

As they left the room, a series of people entered. Each of them familiar. All the loved ones and friends I'd met throughout my journey had returned, and I knew they were there to usher me from this life to the next.

Whatever that may be.

"Ready?"

I looked at the beast, wishing I wasn't.

"Yes."

"Then, let's go."

I climbed from the hospital bed, as though I'd never been sick.

My chest burned and ached as I moved away from the frail body I was leaving. My lungs protested, struggling to work without the machines at first, but within a few feet, they felt the best they'd felt in years.

At the door to my room, I paused and looked back, watching as I took my final breath.

My wife was there, as was my son, and all the memories we'd shared swirled from my body before floating over them, falling like rain so they could absorb each drop.

I followed the beast out, into a dark hallway, towards a light that shone far off in the distance. At first it seemed to blink and flash, before I realized it was the light from the top of the Lighthouse.

In my hospital room, they unhooked the wires and tubes and wheeled my bed away.

Not long after the space was cleaned, a bed returned, and a new patient arrived.

And what were my last thoughts before the darkness disappeared and the shining sea arrived?

Well, to tell you the truth, it was that I knew I hadn't given up. My body had reached its end and there was nothing more I could do. I'd live on.

In the hearts of my wife and my son, I'd live on.

And I'd never be forgotten.

Neither will you.

END

Afterword

So, how're we all doing?

Back in 2017, I released my first novel, 'Invisible.' It took me a long time to write it. Like, a decade. I started and stopped a bunch, finding a groove here, inspiration there and ultimately, when my time as an athlete ended and I turned to writing to keep me going, I released 'Invisible.' Originally, it had a cover of a broken tree on it. I took the photo while camping and it worked well for the sentiment of the story. This broken man fleeing across this nightmarish landscape. I loved the image, but I'm no cover designer.

I'm also no editor. So, I hired an editor who edited it, and they (wrongly) also gave me some literary advice. You see, in the original version of this book, I referenced – both obviously and not – about one hundred songs through lyrics and descriptions. And they told me that as long as I listed them in the back and gave note of their copyright status, I could freely use them.

Yeah, I know.

As it turned out, the editing job they did was horrible as well.

So, I re-edited it myself in 2018, had Mason McDonald do a new cover and re-released it. But I still believed I could use the songs and blah blah blah. It wasn't right. A few years back, I received a review that said something close to this – 'Wonderful book, great sentiments and made me cry, but the editing is trash.' I knew it was true.

Part of it was that I didn't have an editor I trusted. And part of it was that I wasn't a good enough writer to write the book how I felt it should read.

Around that time, I connected with David Sodergren. He's since edited all my work and is a fundamental reason why anyone reads my stuff and enjoys it. He's a significantly better author than I am, and with him in my corner, I knew at some point I wanted to revisit this and give it the justice it deserved.

Which brings me to what you just read.

First – the title change. From 'Invisible' to 'The Invisible.' Why? I wanted a fresh start completely for this one.

As for the subject matter. Well, the entirety that my grandma, Marion Marshall, was alive during my life, she had MS. I only have one memory of her walking and honestly at this point, I don't know if I actually remember her walking or if that's just what my brain has formulated as my memory.

As well, my aunt developed Cancer and passed on very quickly from initial diagnosis to death. She kept it secret for a few months, but it got to a point where it couldn't be hidden anymore and by then we were on borrowed time.

The initial idea for this story germinated when I said my goodbyes to my aunt.

On the drive to the airport, CCR's 'Have You Ever Seen the Rain?' played on the radio. And again, in the airport. And again, in the car ride from the airport to their home. And again, at the hospital. And again, and again and again.

Hearing that song so much, at that moment, formulated some of the story. Of a person, unable to leave the hospital who sees and hears things that are from the hospital, but their brain processes it as something else. The Lighthouse being their room. The car being their wheelchair. The beast being the disease within them. The calendar not making sense because they don't always see it and the days flow together. The gas station representing the cafeteria and so on.

I wanted to write a novel about a person coming to realize that they're dying and not being able to do anything about it.

And because I wanted this to help me accept and understand my own feelings on the subject, I decided to make it both a mix of non-fiction and fiction. Since this was unpublished, I've released my memoir, 'The Color of Melancholy,' so some of this might seem familiar if you've read that.

As well, since unpublishing this and re-writing it, a few other things have happened that made revisiting this book difficult. The two biggest ones were that our beloved dog, OJ, passed away. OJ was our first kid, the biggest goofball and even now, almost three years since he's left us, we talk about him every day and my son misses him dearly. If you've seen the dedication at the start of my novel 'Mastodon,' you'll know just how much we loved him.

And a good friend of ours, Simon Dunn, also passed away. I'd actually forgotten that I had him in this book and when I got to that part I had to pause. Simon was an athlete, an activist, and a Gay Icon to those who simply knew him as those. But to us, he was a dear friend, a loving person, and someone we'd hoped to have in our lives forever.

We miss both of them so much.

Other things have happened too, but I'm not going to go down the rabbit hole of sorrow here, if you want to find those out, check out my memoir!

Now, for the thanks.

First, thank you to Mason McDonald for your prior cover help and support! To Justin M. Woodward – you hailed this novel back in the day even when it was poorly written, and your support and friendship have always meant so much. A.A. Medina. Thank you for the new awesome cover that perfectly nails this story. I'm always in awe of what you create. If you've note read Medina's fiction as well, definitely go read his work! Jeremy Hepler! Thank you for your friendship and giving this a read and providing the foreword! Your novel, 'The Boulevard Monster' is one of the best books I've ever read and 'Cricket Hunters' and 'Sunray Alice' are just as phenomenal.

To those authors who are always there to show support (I'm gonna forget folks, so apologies!) – Laurel Hightower, Sonora Taylor, V. Castro, J.H. Moncrieff, J.R. McConvey, Duncan Ralston, Zachary Ashford, Chris & Jay & Little Ghosts, Cindy O'Quinn, Tim McGregor, Robert P. Ottone, Matt and Alex at Tenebrous, Espen Aukan (and Stine!), Ronald McGillvray, Naben Ruthnum, Andrew F. Sullivan, David Demchuk, Geneve Flynn, Chris Marrs, Craig DiLouie, Dave Jeffery, Adam Nevill, J.A. Sullivan, Matt Wildasin, Kev Harrison, BP Gregory, Erin Al-Mehairi, Brennan Storr, Michael Wehunt, Joseph Sale, RJ Roles, Matthew Vaughn, Brennan LaFaro, Michelle River, Yolanda Sfetsos, C.M Forest and so many, many, many more! Thank you all!

Thank you to the constant support of Kiera (thathorrorbish), Alexia(miss_kittie_frantastico), V (slow_reading_with_v), Deb (dlgillis20), Dustin Ekman, Gavin at Kendall Reviews, and so many other book readers and reviewers who've been there to support my work, but also always sending me funny stuff!

Huge thanks to my Patreon crew – Kiera, Alexia, David, Brett Plaxton, James Pare, exhaustedtech, Ted Campiso Jr. Ally Rhodes, Clive Viagas, Tracey Nudd with Twizted Talez Publicationz, Jay D., Matt McCleland, Geoff Parrell, Hughes Ouimet, MJ., Rob Jeromson, Jay Bower, Emma Roantree, Derek Gottlieb, Lauren K, Jodi Stredulinsky, Bob P., and Emily Blackwell! You're kindness and support have been amazing!

Andrew Pyper. I started this book before I found 'The Demonologist.' But it was discovering 'The Demonologist' that kicked me in the pants and suggested that maybe this Canadian kid could write something people might want to read. Your kindness and friendship mean more than I can ever adequately express. Thank you.

David Sodergren. Thank you for your friendship, support and editing prowess. You've been there far longer than many, and you always work hard to make sure I deliver the best product I can. To see that you've now been able to transition into a full-time writer makes me so proud and so happy.

And thank you to Amanda and Auryn.

If it weren't for you two, I'd be lost. You make every day brighter. I love you both.

Seriously, thank you for all reading this.

Revisiting this and rewriting it has been the most difficult thing I've done in some time.

But it's been completely worth it.

Until we meet again.

Steve

August 14th, 2024

Edmonton, Alberta.

About the Author

A multiple-award nominated author, Steve Stred lives in Edmonton, Alberta, Canada, with his wife and son.

Known for his novels, 'Mastodon,' 'Churn the Soil,' and his series 'Father of Lies' where he joined a cult on the dark web for four years, his work has been described as haunting, bleak and is frequently set in the woods near where he grew up. He's been fortunate to appear in numerous anthologies with some truly amazing authors.

His novel 'Mastodon' will be translated into Czech and Italian over the next few years.

He is an Active Member of the HWA.

For TV/Film Rights, please email Alec Frankel at afrankel@ independentartistgroup.com

To find more of his work, please visit his website
– stevestredauthor.ca